Catching Her Bear

Weres & Witches of Silver Lake
Book 2

Vella Day

Copyright © 2016 Vella Day

CATCHING HER BEAR
Copyright © 2016 by Vella Day
Print Edition
www.velladay.com
velladayauthor@gmail.com

Cover Art by Jaycee DeLorenzo
Edited by Rebecca Cartee and Carol Adcock-Bezzo

Published in the United States of America

E-book ISBN: 978-1-941835-21-0
Print book ISBN: 978-1-941835-22-7

ALL RIGHTS RESERVED. No part of this book may be used or reproduced in any manner whatsoever without written permission of the author except in the case of brief questions embodied in critical articles or reviews.

This is a work of fiction. Names, characters, places, and incidents either are the product of the author's imagination or are used fictitiously, and any resemblance to actual persons living or dead, business establishments, events or locales, is entirely coincidental.

Beneath the calm and shimmering surface lie intrigue, power, magic, and danger.
Welcome to Silver Lake—where appearances can be deceiving, and what you see isn't truly what lies below.

Chapter One

Brother Jacob stood behind the hand carved table on the raised platform and shut the lid to his laptop. He then held up his hand to quiet the Changeling Council members sitting on unforgiving wooden chairs before him. The dim lights flickering from the six gas sconces barely illuminated their faces, and the black wool curtains covering the cement walls added the air of mystery and secrecy.

Once the ten-member group settled, he glanced at the two new room additions that he'd personally commissioned. Fine pieces of work. The two statues had a human bottom half, but from the shoulders up, they were pure Changeling wolf, complete with red onyx eyes that were lit from behind.

He returned his attention to his men whose eyes were focused solely on him. Three of the members had failed to don their robes. They would suffer for that slight.

Using his most commanding Alpha tone, he addressed. "Brother Chris, tell us that you've procured the sardonyx."

This blood colored stone, when imbued with a powerful curse could extract the powers from a Wendayan. On the red moon, this magic could be transferred to one of them. The Changelings could dominate all of Silver Lake and beyond if they were able to harness the witches' magic.

"Not yet, Brother Jacob. The Stanleys are claiming that the Indian mine where they found the last shipment of stone is now closed, but they are scouring the world for another source. As you know, that particular red stone is difficult to locate."

Jacob slammed his hand on the table, the sound reverberating in the small room. "Unacceptable! Tell them they have one week or they die." He didn't bother wiping the spittle from his chin.

"Yes, Brother Jacob."

KALAN MURDOCH, THE werebear Beta of the shifter Clan of wolves and bears, sat in his Alpha's living room, pad of paper in hand, discussing their duties as newly appointed leaders in Silver Lake, Tennessee. Even at ten in the morning, his eyes were tired from taking notes, and the strong coffee Rye's mate had made for them didn't seem to be working at all.

Right after Izzy had moved in, she'd placed a lamp next to the lounge chair, but even that didn't provide enough light to see well. He did appreciate the added crystals, colorful candles in all shapes and sizes, and some much needed throw pillows, like the one supporting his back to the stark black leather décor from before.

Kalan pointed his pen at Rye. "Here's a thought. We could exact enough pink quartz from the bottom of the lake to give a piece to everyone." The recent rash of robberies and fires had alarmed some of the members, and the quartz would provide a modicum of protection against the evil and ever illusive Changelings. Personally, he'd never used the stuff, but rumor had it that great power resided in the quartz.

Ryerson McKinnon, his Alpha, propped his feet on the wooden coffee table. "It's not like it's their Kryptonite. Only a massive amount of the stone from the bottom of Silver Lake seems to disrupt the Changelings' powers whenever they enter our land."

"Do you think something the size of Izzy's quartz crystals would have an effect on one of them?" He bet that if a Changeling ever walked into this room, he would definitely feel his powers drained immediately.

"I doubt it, which is why we need to get closer to them and find out what they're up to. Stop them before they can do more damage. You're the cop. There has to be something you can do."

"Not without attracting attention." The sheriff wasn't even aware shifters existed, so Kalan wouldn't be getting any support from his department. "Perhaps James can help."

James was their resident immortal and husband to their moon goddess, Naliana. He had a Changeling contact who had previously helped in locating Izzy after that Scottish Changeling had come to capture Rye's mate.

"I don't want to rely on him for everything," Rye said.

"Asking for help a few times isn't exactly relying on him. If you don't want to go that route, what do you propose?" Kalan asked.

"Not sure. Izzy might have been joking at the time, but she suggested we find someone to go undercover to infiltrate their ranks."

Kalan laughed. "Right, that would be a death sentence."

"Not if we hire an out-of-towner, someone who has experience working with Changelings."

"Good luck finding him. Our kind doesn't exactly advertise in the Yellow Pages."

"I can be patient." Rye leaned forward, snatched his cup off the table, and tipped it back. "Did I mention Izzy's birthday is in two days, and that we're going to have a little get together here this weekend?"

Kalan had to assume the discussion about how to handle the Changelings was now closed, so he tossed the pad at his feet. "No. Then again, you've been a bit preoccupied."

His best friend grinned. "I'm telling you, having Izzy in my life has been the best thing that has ever happened to me."

Kalan could tell where this conversation was going, and he needed to nip it in the bud. "I'm happy the two of you are mated, but just so you know, I'm perfectly content being single." As a deputy and part time detective in the criminal division of the sheriff's

3

department, he worked erratic hours. Sampling the women of Silver Lake whenever the need arose worked perfectly for his lifestyle. More importantly, now that he was the new Beta of the large Clan, he didn't need to be tied down. "What can I bring to the party?"

"Nothing. I'm barbequing some burgers and stuff. I think Izzy's mom and sister are doing the rest."

Kalan wasn't the type to arrive empty-handed. He'd at least buy Izzy a gift. Easing off the lounge chair, he grabbed his empty coffee cup, walked over to the kitchen, and set it in the sink. "Gotta get back to work." Before taking a step, his cell rang and he checked the caller ID. "Speak of the devil."

Rye stood. "Go ahead and answer it. If our paths don't cross beforehand, I'll see you Saturday."

"You got it."

As Kalan left Rye's, he answered his phone. "Murdoch."

"It's Phil." Phil Smythe was his boss and the head of the Criminal Division.

"I was just on my way in," Kalan said.

While the day was overcast, the warm late summer air was scented with the sweet aroma of pine from the surrounding forest.

"Good, but first I need you to run down a lead. It's regarding the Donaldson warehouse fire. When we brought in the owner last month, he claimed he was at a church social that night, but now a witness has come forward who puts him someplace else. I need you to speak with the pastor for confirmation."

"I'll check it out."

Kalan hopped in his freshly washed Jeep and headed into town. As he passed the colorfully painted Blooms of Hope flower shop, located across the street from where Izzy worked, an idea popped into his head. He'd check out the lead then buy Izzy a birthday bouquet. That seemed like a safe gift. Women liked flowers, and he'd been told it stayed fresh for a couple of days at least.

On the edge of town, Kalan parked in front of Hope Church, a white wooden structure graced with a tall, beautiful spire. From the outside, it looked pious as hell, especially with the stone statue garden off to the side that included the heavenly family and a host of other saints. He'd always wondered if he hadn't met a real goddess, what his belief system might have been. Now wasn't the time, however, to debate the validity of religion.

He eased out of his Jeep. Not wanting to be disrespectful, he drew back his wavy locks and secured it with a rubber band before heading inside. His eyes quickly adjusted to the low light, most of which was coming from the beautiful stained glass window above the altar. Kalan inhaled the rich scent of fresh furniture polish and let his muscles relax.

He had to admit the cushions on the wooden pews made it rather homey. No one was inside praying, or whatever a person did inside a church, but he had to believe the pastor was around somewhere.

Thinking that the door off to the side of the rather austere altar might house some offices, Kalan went in search of the man. After passing a series of religious photos on the wall, Kalan located him at the end of the hallway.

The door to his office sat ajar, and a man wearing glasses and a buttoned down shirt was sitting at his desk. Kalan knocked and entered. "Excuse me." He held up his badge.

The pastor slipped off his glasses and set them down, shoved back his chair, and then stood. "Yes, officer, how may I help you?"

"I need to ask you about one of your parishioners, a Jack Donaldson."

"What about him?" His tone, along with slightly pinched lips, implied he was ready to defend the man at any cost.

"I need to know whether or not he was at your church social on the 13th of last month."

"He most certainly was. In fact, I spoke with him about his daughter."

"What time was that?"

The pastor ran a hand over his chin. "I can't say when our conversation occurred exactly, but the social ran from six to nine, and Jack Donaldson was here the whole time. He's such a wonderful man. Never misses church."

Well, that was a bust. The fire department said the blaze had been set around seven. Not that Kalan thought the pastor would lie, but to be thorough he wanted to touch base with a few others as well as the eyewitness who put Donaldson someplace else. "Do you have a list of the guests who attended?"

"They all signed in. If you give me a moment, I'll make you a copy."

"That would be great. Thanks."

The pastor pulled open a desk drawer and extracted a book. He then made a photocopy on his scanner and printed it. "Here you go."

Jeez. It was three pages of names. "Appreciate it."

"Any time. Say, I haven't seen you in church."

"Been busy," Kalan replied. He didn't want to discuss his habits and waved the papers. "Best be going. Thanks again."

"Come again soon, son."

Kalan didn't respond. He glanced down at the papers again and hoped one of these names could provide a lead. Because most of these folks would be at work for another few hours, he decided to purchase the flowers for Izzy then head into the station.

As he drove closer to the Blooms of Hope flower shop, a parking space freed up in front, which he considered good karma. Passing the display window before the entrance, he stopped, spotting the perfect gift for Izzy. It was a vase of pink, red, white, and orange wild flowers behind a cute stuffed wolf. Izzy and her wild, magical ways would love it. That was the easiest present he'd ever found.

When he stepped inside the fragrant smelling shop to purchase the gift, the ease he'd just experienced totally disappeared. His heart fluttered and his incisors lengthened. Holy shit. He didn't detect a shifter close by, so there was no need for his body to go into fight mode. Something was seriously wrong.

Behind the counter stood a woman about twenty-five or so, with her hair in a braid and more tattoos on her arm than there were flowers in the shop. She was placing pink roses in a long box for a customer. Nothing about that should have triggered his unwanted reaction. A large glass cooler filled with flowers of every kind lined one wall, but as a bear shifter, he wasn't allergic to anything relating to the outdoors, so he shouldn't be feeling light-headed.

The clerk packaging the flowers for the customer turned her head toward the back. "Elana, customer," she called.

Elana, Elana. He mentally snapped his fingers. Izzy's friend was named Elana. When he was at the Emergency Room the day Rye had been injured, he'd also had a strange feeling he couldn't identify. His only thought at the time was that he had to get out of the waiting room. Hell, he'd been so flustered he'd walked right into the closed glass door.

"Hello," Elana said, stepping out from the back, her voice like a smooth malt whiskey.

Dark hair with hints of red lay around her shoulders. This time she'd let it hang loose instead of pulling it back in a ponytail, and boy what a difference that made. Her soft, blue eyes looked dreamy, almost as if she'd been sniffing too many flowers or something and had gotten high.

His heart nearly stopped when his eyes lowered to her perfect pink lips, the exact shade as the rose petals her assistant was stuffing into the cardboard box. As he let his gaze roam from her eyes, over her chest, and then down to her legs and back up to her face again, his nails began to grow and it totally freaked him out. What the hell was wrong with him? She was a mere human.

But what man or rather shifter could resist drinking her in? The top of her head was no higher than his chest, and her tits looked to be about a D cup, enough to fill his big hands. And her lush hips? Man, they were made to cradle a man in ecstasy.

Where the hell did those thoughts come from?

Say something, you oaf. "Hey there. Remember me? Kalan Murdoch. I'm Rye's friend."

"Oh, sure. Elana Stanley."

They shook hands, and the second he touched her, his bear went crazy, screaming *mate, mate.*

Kalan had no idea where he came up with that idea. A human who wasn't a Wendayan could never be his mate.

"When Rye was released from the hospital I, ah, heard you gave him a lift back," Kalan said. "That was really nice of you. Just so you don't think I'm a jerk, I would have driven him but I was called back to work." *Babble, babble...*

That was bull and totally lame. He hadn't even received or made a call when he was there.

"Thanks. I heard he's doing well."

"He is." Kalan might have elaborated, but every word in his head seemed to have evaporated. Even concentrating took effort.

Focus.

He couldn't. Something was happening that scared the shit out of him. Kalan Murdoch was always in control—unless he was in the presence of Elana it seemed.

"Are you here for some flowers?"

"Flowers, yes. I saw a display in the window along with a stuffed wolf that would make a perfect gift."

She smiled, but her eyes didn't light up. In fact, she appeared to be in pain. For the life of him, he couldn't think of what he'd said to make her so sad.

"The ones with the wild flowers?"

"Yes."

"I'll make one up for you."

He wanted to say he'd take the one in the window as that would hurry things along, but when she rushed over to the flower cooler, he didn't want to make things worse for her. As soon as the first customer left the store, the girl working the register stepped into the back. Alone with Elana, his senses heightened. Kalan placed a hand to his forehead thinking he might be coming down with something.

Elana carried the fresh flowers and vase to the counter and began to arrange them. Mesmerized by her agility and care, Kalan slowly lifted his gaze to her face. While not classically beautiful, Elana Stanley was a striking woman who made his libido pound with unwanted desire—or at least it was unwanted at the moment.

"Here's the wolf," the clerk said waving the stuffed animal. "You want me to ring him up, Elana?"

Her smile seemed to wobble. "Sure."

It then hit him like a stampede of wild boar. "You're friends with Izzy. Do you think she'll like this for her birthday?"

As if the sun peaked out from the clouds, she grinned. "Absolutely. In fact, a while ago, she was admiring the one in the window."

Relieved he'd picked out something his Alpha's mate would like, he withdrew his credit card and handed it to the tattooed girl at the counter.

"Are you going to Izzy's birthday party?" he asked. She was Izzy's best friend, so it made sense she would be.

"Yes, are you?"

He had come in for a present, but he could always say he'd purchased the gift because he couldn't make it. "I'm hoping to. I work long hours, and I get called into work all the time."

He didn't want Elana to think he was looking to hook up. Given she was Izzy's best friend, he wouldn't even chance asking her out, not even to the movies. It could only end in disaster.

She set the bouquet and wolf on the counter. "Here you go. We're open Saturday until noon. If you stop in, I'll give you a helium balloon to attach to the vase."

Elana was too nice. "If I have time, I will, thanks."

Kalan couldn't wait to leave. He was battling this unwanted attraction again, and if he shifted in a public place, the world would never be the same. As soon as he signed his name, he swiped the vase of flowers and wolf off the counter and rushed out. Just he reached the door, the stuffed animal slipped from his fingers and dropped. He fumbled to pick it up and then bumped his head on the door handle as he stood up. Damn. He swore Elana giggled.

Face heating, he tucked the wolf under his arm while he opened the door and hurried out. No way in hell he was going to that party and subject himself to being near her again.

Chapter Two

Elana sat alone in a booth at McKinnon's Pub and Pool waiting for her friends to arrive for happy hour. The floor was littered with peanut shells, but that was what gave the place the cozy, family-friendly vibe, or else it was the polished bar and the spotless mirror above that made her feel the pub was clean and safe.

Even though it wasn't too noisy yet, she'd picked a booth in the back of the main area, far away from the pool room, as shouts occasionally came from there.

Elana couldn't wait to share her hot news with her friends. Her body was still zinging from being in Kalan Murdoch's presence for so long yesterday. At least she hadn't made a fool of herself, though she must have done something to make the hunky man so nervous.

The whole time he'd been standing there, she'd tried to keep her fingers from shaking as she arranged the flowers, when what she really wanted to do was run her fingers through those dirty blond curls of his. The shoulder-length locks made him look rugged and romantic. Coupled with the slight scruff on his face and those full, kissable lips, Kalan was her dream man.

Since Izzy would be at happy hour this time, Elana would have to alter her story a bit as to why Kalan had come into her store. She'd have to say he was there to buy some roses for his mom or something, though the truth would come out as soon as her friend saw the wild flowers and stuffed wolf at her party.

Since sitting alone made her a bit self-conscious, Elana checked out the menu, her mouth watering at the pictures of the juicy hamburgers, fries, and thick steaks. It didn't matter she'd already eaten.

Elana probably shouldn't have come so early, but she'd wanted to make sure they had a booth. She'd only been to McKinnon's Pub once before and didn't know how busy it would be on a Thursday night. She, Missy, and Teagan used to meet down the street at the Lake Steakhouse bar, but now that Izzy was back in town, she wanted to come here, probably because Rye's uncle owned the place.

The door opened and her three friends came in, lowering her anxiety level. Elana smiled and waved as they all rushed over. One by one, they hugged her. Izzy and Missy sat across from her and Teagan slid in next to her.

Within seconds, their waitress, a girl she'd known slightly in high school, came over asking for their drink orders. Elana wasn't much of a drinker. Not only did one or two glasses make her tipsy, she couldn't afford the weight gain from the alcohol. If she had any hope of ever catching Kalan Murdoch's eye, she'd have to slim down, though that was the story of her life. It seemed like she'd been on an endless diet for the last ten years.

"Elana?" asked Izzy.

She looked up. "What?"

The girls chuckled. "Molly just asked what you'd like to drink."

Oh, crap. She'd been daydreaming about Kalan. "I'll have your house Merlot, please." Damn, and here she was just telling herself not to drink. Oh, well. She'd give up dessert tomorrow.

Molly nodded and left. Apparently, her friends had given her their order already. Sheesh. Elana inhaled, needing to share her news and ask for advice. "You'll never guess who came into my flower shop."

The girls exchanged glances. "Who?" Missy asked.

"Kalan Murdoch."

Izzy leaned forward then flipped her long hair over her shoulder. "Kalan came to the flower shop? Why?"

She let loose her little fib. "He was buying something for his mom. I think it was her birthday."

"Aw, that is sweet. He's coming over on Saturday to my birthday party, you know," Izzy said.

She shook her head. "He said he might have to work."

One brow rose. "He said that?"

Elana didn't like her tone. Oh, shit. If they were discussing Izzy's party, she might think he was in the store to buy something for her. "Yes."

Izzy shook her head. "He'll be there. He's Rye's best friend, and I don't think Rye would forgive him if he didn't come."

"I hope so." Elana tried not to let the relief show, but a grin crept up on her face anyway. "What are you all wearing?"

Missy shrugged. "I'm just wearing jeans and a T-shirt. It's more or less an outside affair."

Darn. "I guess heels are out then. I hate being the shortest one around."

Teagan clasped her hand. "Don't tell me you're interested in Kalan?"

She didn't know why Teagan sounded so surprised. Elana twisted in her seat. "I admit he's a little older, but he's so fucking hot!" The group laughed and she slumped against her seat. "He's out of my league, isn't he? I'm stupid for thinking about him."

"No," they all said in unison.

Their drinks arrived—her red wine, Izzy's white one, and two colorful Mojitos, full of mint and lime, for Missy and Teagan. Elana tipped back half her glass. Fortunately, no one commented.

Izzy waved a hand. "Forget him. Kalan doesn't deserve you. When he's not on the job, he plays around—or so Rye said. You can do better."

"That's sweet of you to say, but I want to give him a chance." She'd watched him for years now but never had the nerve to speak with him. When she ran into him at the hospital after checking up on Rye, he'd seemed out of sorts. When he suddenly said he had to leave right away and then ran right into the door, it almost looked like he was trying to get away from her as quickly as possible. She hoped there had been another explanation.

Missy lifted her refreshing looking drink. "I have a kickass top you can borrow, if you want. It will really show off your tits."

Elana almost spit out her wine. "I don't want to lure him in like that."

Missy shook her head. "It's called advertising. You have to get him to look first before buying. Then he'll find out how incredible you are."

"Real incredible." *Not.*

Teagan chimed in. "How many women have started a business? Huh?"

"My parents are the consummate entrepreneurs. I learned from them."

Izzy glanced to the ceiling. "You barely saw them. It's not like they took you anywhere to show you what they did for a living."

A sharp pain stabbed her just below her heart. "I heard all about their adventures when they came home." She would have learned more if her parents had taken her on even one of their worldwide jaunts.

"Where did they go this last time?" Izzy asked.

Clearly, her best friend had read the longing on Elana's face and felt bad about it. Understandably, Izzy never had any use for her mom and dad since they often neglected her. "India."

Teagan sipped her drink. "How exotic. Were they there to buy stuff for their import-export company?"

How sad that they hadn't discussed anything with her in the last few years. "I don't know, but that's what I'm guessing." Elana didn't want this get together to be about her. "Anyone else have news?"

Izzy's face brightened, clearly knowing why Elana wanted to change the subject. When they were in school, Izzy had been furious that Elana's parents left for weeks on end, leaving her with just the hired help.

Izzy waved a hand. "I do. I have a teaching job!"

From Missy and Teagan's expression, they already knew this piece of information. "When did you hear?"

"About an hour ago. I wanted to surprise you."

"You did." Her spirits rose with excitement for her best friend. "Are you teaching Chemistry?"

"Yes, at Hanerford's Private School."

The girls oohed at hearing the name of the prestigious place. She and Izzy had attended the local public school. Then they discussed what Izzy knew about her class size and the course content and details. When she'd told them as much as she knew, the talk returned to the upcoming birthday bash.

Elana turned to Teagan. "Are you bringing Kip to the party?"

She shrugged. "I don't think so."

Elana waited for her to elaborate, but she didn't. Kip worked for Rye's brother, so there was no reason not to go, unless…

Not wanting to touch that topic, she glanced at a group of rowdy men who'd just waltzed in, seemingly fresh off some construction site. Elana sighed, loving how so many people came just to hang out with friends. She had a lonely childhood until she started school and met Izzy, and then eventually became friends with Missy and Teagan. She was thankful every day for having her best friends.

For the rest of their get together, they focused on good news, like about how happy Izzy was with Rye. "Because of my talents," Izzy explained, "I kept to myself a lot. For the longest time, I never thought I'd want to settle down with one person. Then I met Rye."

That was so sweet. Elana had dreamed of being with one man her whole life. At twenty-seven, she wasn't certain she'd ever find anyone who wanted her as much as she wanted him.

Before they had the chance to order a second round, Izzy said she needed to return home and help clean up for the party. Elana suspected it was because her urges were acting up again. She'd confided in Elana that once she and Rye had mated, her sex drive had been out of control.

Elana wondered if their weekly time together would soon become a once a month and then an every other month thing. At least Missy was single with no boyfriend in sight.

They waved for their checks and paid. These girls were lucky. They had special powers—something any man would be attracted to. Elana didn't even have any money in the bank. Everything she earned, she plowed back into the business.

In the parking lot, they said their goodbyes saying they'd see each other at the party. As the three of them drove away, a feeling of melancholy descended at being alone. In a way, Elana had done it to herself by spending all her time working and building her flower business. But that was going to change. After the way her heart beat so hard when she spoke with Kalan at the hospital and again at the store, she had a new mission—to land Kalan Murdoch.

KALAN ENTERED RYE'S house on Saturday a little bit before the party was to begin and was pleased Izzy wasn't in sight. Wanting to keep the present a surprise, he hid it behind one of the chairs in the living room. Kalan had casually mentioned to Rye that he might not be able to attend Izzy's party as there was a lot going on at work. Unfortunately, his best friend told him that was a bullshit excuse, that if he wanted to remain the Beta of the Clan, he needed to show up. Sometimes it sucked that Rye saw through his lame excuses.

Kalan stepped into the backyard where four tables were covered with colorful cloths, and each had a candle and crystal on top. "Need help?"

"I'm good. Watch this." He turned on the gas in the grill, and when he held out his hand, a small flame shot from his palm, igniting it.

"Good goddess. You're getting a lot better. Last time, you could only do sparks."

Rye grinned. "I know. Still can't make a blade of grass grow, but with enough concentration, I can manage to move a few papers by forcing air under them."

"Perhaps I should hook up with a Wendayan. I wouldn't mind some extra skills."

When he and Izzy, a Wendayan, had mated, she'd inherited his ability to shift, and Rye had been gifted with some of her skills, only on a much smaller scale.

His best friend laughed. "Did it slip your mind that you have to mate with this person first—for life? And you don't get to choose who it is."

Instantly the image of Elana surfaced, but he immediately suppressed it. Not having a choice was the scariest part of this whole mating thing. Even his dad had never been able to explain how or why people were paired.

"There you are." Izzy stepped onto the back patio looking lovely in a white sundress that accentuated her auburn hair. She leaned over and kissed his cheek.

"Happy birthday," Kalan said.

"Thank you. Just as a reminder, you two need to be on your best behavior—or at least you do, Kalan. Our resident human, Elana, will be here."

"She knows Rye is a shifter, right?"

"Yes, but not that anyone else is. I've never even said that bears can shift."

Well, that sucked. So much for cutting loose tonight. The front door bell rang, and Izzy excused herself. Kalan probably should tell Rye about the strange way his body reacted around Elana, but a party wasn't the time or place.

His plan for the party was to spend his time talking to everyone but her. The last thing he needed was for his eyes to glow amber and the hair on his body to sprout. Everyone except Elana would recognize the signs as that of sexual excitement. She'd probably conclude he had some kind of medical condition.

Two women stepped onto the patio along with Izzy's parents. A few months back, Kalan had an aura cleansing from Katherine Berta, so he knew her, but he didn't recognize the others. Izzy introduced them. The one with auburn hair was Missy Berta, Izzy's sister, and the blonde was their cousin Teagan Pompley. Both were attractive girls, but they weren't really his type. He liked his women flashy and sexy with some womanly curves.

The image of Elana's shape blasted through his mind once more, but he shook it off. Did he want to delve into her sweetness? Hell, yeah, but that was all. Love 'em and leave 'em was his motto, but Elana was off limits, plain and simple. Being Izzy's best friend sucked, the fallout if they dated wouldn't be worth it. Keeping it secret from Rye would be impossible too.

Someone pressed a cold beer in his hand. When he focused, he was looking into two beautiful blue eyes—Elana's—and his heart thumped.

"You look like someone died so I thought you could use a drink," she said with just the right mix of humor and sympathy.

He grinned, but inside his gut was doing a tumbling act. His bear wanted to stroke her face and kiss her, but his human had enough sense to know that was totally out of the question. "Thanks. I didn't see you come in."

How hadn't he? She had on a clingy top in the exact color blue as her eyes and smelled like flowers after a soft rain. That alone was making him crazy.

Just being around Elana for the two short times was enough to suspect she wore black jeans to make herself look slimmer. Little did she know that she didn't have to wear a sexy outfit to attract him.

I'll take her just the way she is, his bear commented.

Shut up. Kalan needed to find a way to silent the horny animal clawing his way to get out.

She'd pulled her hair back from her face with some kind of clip, and the overall impression made every inch of his body stand up and take notice. Damn cock. He twisted to help correct the discomfort.

"I'm stealthy like that." She lifted her chin, looking defiant, but most likely it was to meet his gaze.

"Good comeback." He liked Elana and didn't want to hurt her, so he wouldn't make up some lame excuse why he had to step away and help Rye with dinner.

His gaze then left her lovely face and traced a path down to her large breasts. He had no control over his expression. His eyes widened on their own and then a few of his bones cracked. Crap. Kalan looked to the side and chugged a good portion of his beer, searching for control. If his bear didn't get a grip, something bad might happen.

Elana placed a hand on his arm and things went from passable to worse. "Are you okay?"

This time he didn't lie. "I'm not feeling all that well. Can you excuse me?" He touched his face and it appeared warm, though that could be from the summer temperature.

"Sure."

He hadn't meant to bail, but if he shifted in front of a human, it might jeopardize the Clans' peaceful existence. Kalan tossed back the rest of his drink, dashed inside, and headed to the fridge for another one, passing the coffee table that was laden with gifts for Izzy.

Something was going on with him, but he wasn't about to ask Rye what it might be. Because Rye had just found his mate, he'd claim Elana was his. Right, a human. No way.

Mate, mate.

He refused to listen. All he could think of was that Naliana was bored and wanted to fuck with him. *Welcome to being a Beta. I've thrown a hot chick your way to see what you would do. It's a test to see if you can resist her. I'll make her totally desirable to ensure that you're made of sterner stuff.*

Naliana could take her test and shove it up her ass—no disrespect meant. Kalan wasn't going to let his dick rule and ruin his good life.

A few more people arrived and he greeted them, happy his body had finally calmed down. Most were wolf shifters, but a few of the bears had shown up too. Izzy had been out of the country for so long that her roots weren't deep anymore, so none of her old high school friends had been invited, which was probably for the best. They didn't need anyone to slip and mention shifters.

Elana was the only human at the party who wasn't a witch, and while she was aware shifters existed and had seen Izzy's powers, she was basically in the dark about the rest.

He almost chuckled thinking how she'd freak if he shifted in front of her. Of course, he'd never do that to her, but if he filmed it—which he never would—he bet he'd get a billion hits on YouTube.

"There you are." Elana stepped close.

This was the second time he'd not sensed she was near. He knew why. He'd been so distracted thinking about her that all his other senses had zoned out—even his acute sense of smell. When her delicate rose like scent seeped into him again, his stupid body reacted by growing unwanted hair on his arms and probably his face. Kalan hadn't pulled his almost shoulder length hair back in a tie, and right now, he probably looked like a bear.

He needed something to focus on other than what her presence was doing to him. If she hadn't had a drink in her hand, he would have offered her one. Fortunately, he was provided with a distraction when the crowd piled into the living room.

"Are they coming in to open the presents?" he asked. *Please say yes.*

"Yes, presents first then food."

"Sounds good." In all his years of dating, he didn't remember a more awkward situation. His body was clamoring to be with her, yet his mind was sending out strong warning signals to stay away. Kalan had this impending sense that once he gave into his inner bear he'd never be able to escape.

Move you idiot.

"Let's find a seat," he said. Kalan stepped past the chairs and sofa to retrieve his hidden present and placed it with the others on the coffee table.

He'd planned to snag a seat by himself, but when he looked around, Elana was smiling, patting the remaining seat on the sofa. Well, damn.

Chapter Three

"JUST STOP. IT wasn't a disaster," Izzy said as she lifted her iced tea to her lips.

Elana sank back on the sofa in her apartment above the store, exhausted from not having slept a wink last night. Izzy was seated across from her in the flowered wingback chair—a hand-me-down from her parents.

Nothing about Izzy's party had gone according to plan. After sounding rather despondent on the phone, Izzy told her she was coming over to talk her off the ledge. Elana said her situation wasn't that bad, but she was upset with herself. She'd had the chance to make an impression on Kalan, and she'd blown it.

"Tell me this," Elana said. "How come every time Kalan is near me, he tries to get away?" Elana enumerated all the times he'd run from her. "When he ran smack into the hospital door after seeing Rye, I thought it was cute, figuring he was upset over his best friend being trapped in a burning building. Then when he'd purchased the arrangement for you, he didn't hang out and chat. In fact, he moved so fast, he dropped the wolf on his way out the door and bumped his head." Izzy opened her mouth, but Elana held up her hand. She needed to make sure Izzy understood the extent of the situation. "At your party, he was making one excuse after another why he had to get away from me. I just need to take the hint and move on."

Izzy set her drink down. "I'm not in his head, but maybe he's scared."

Elana cracked up. "Yes, as well he should be. Why my black belt in karate would make any man shake in his boots." Hell, she hadn't stepped foot in a gym in her entire life, let alone hold a beginner's belt in martial arts. She stood. "I need a drink."

In ten steps, she was in her open floor plan kitchen. Instead of pouring an iced tea for herself, she fixed a glass of wine. So what if it was early afternoon?

When she returned, Izzy had a scowl on her face. "You never drink during the day."

"I'm upset."

"He might ask you out. You never know. The party was just last night."

After taking a long swig, Elana set down her glass, and tilted her head. "Really? Why would he do that? He's not interested, and I just need to get it into my head that I have to look elsewhere." She'd tried. Oh, how she'd tried.

Izzy snapped her fingers. "I know. We'll ask Ophelia to put a love spell on Kalan."

Elana held up her palms. "No offense to your kind, but while I know you have magic because I've witnessed it, I'm not so much a believer in love spells."

"Don't be such a skeptic. They can work."

"Is that what you used with Rye?"

Her friend glanced to the side. "No. He seemed to recognize that I was his mate from the get go."

She'd heard that shifters had this intense and almost violent longing to be with their fated mate. Too bad human men weren't the same. "So basically you're suggesting I try to fool Kalan into falling for me?"

"It's not fooling. He'll pursue you, recognize what a catch you are, and then the two of you will fall madly in love on your own."

"If you say so, but remember the spell that crazy witch put on you only lasted forty-eight hours. Is that all the time I'd have to convince him I'm wonderful?" Elana disliked sarcasm, but at the moment, she couldn't help it.

Izzy leaned back and shot her a knowing glance. "It's more like a week to ten days for a love spell. Listen, if you don't act like you're worth fighting for, why should he believe you are?"

Even though she was on the second floor, a motorcycle roared up the street below and rattled her windows. "What are you saying?"

"You need to have faith that if you and Kalan are meant to be together, things will work out. Whether or not it does, is a different matter. It's all about attitude. Men can sense when you're desperate."

She wasn't desperate. Or was she? "I've never claimed we are each other's destiny. I just want one date."

Izzy tossed her a knowing smile. "One date, huh? Or what he has to offer in bed?"

"I'll need the date first before I can land him in bed."

"Then ask him out. This is the twenty-first century. Women do it all the time."

She shook her head. "I'm not sure I could handle it if he said no. It might be best if I had a spell to convince me that Kalan is *not* the one. Let's be honest. Men like Kalan don't go out with someone like me."

Izzy's lips couldn't have puckered any more than if she'd eaten a lemon. "If that's what you truly believe, I'm sure I can arrange a spell to eliminate your desire for Kalan Murdoch from your brain. That kind of spell is definitely in Ophelia's wheel house."

Izzy was suddenly being very cooperative, and the look of sincerity implied she'd do her best. "Thank you. I need to focus on my work and not on having a record number of climaxes."

"To be clear, you want to erase him from your head since you know it can't be any more than that, right?"

"Is that what I said? Maybe. Kind of. Aw, hell, I don't know what I want." *Besides Kalan.*

Izzy thankfully laughed. "I can see that. Before you dismiss it altogether, there's a lot to be said for hot sex."

"Uh-huh." The discussion needed to end now. "When can you

arrange for this dismissal spell?"

Izzy stood. "I'll try to find Ophelia now. If she can do it this afternoon, are you willing to meet me at my old house?"

"Absolutely."

They hugged goodbye. As soon as Izzy left, Elana headed downstairs to her closed flower shop. The delightful scent of the blooming flowers along with the cheery balloons and holiday cards on the wall rack brought her joy. She couldn't imagine doing anything else other than being a florist.

Determined to keep busy until Izzy contacted her, Elana checked her delivery schedule and what arrangements she had to make and for when. She was in the middle of placing some white roses in a vase when her cell rang. It was Izzy.

"Hello, my spell binding witch." She smiled and leaned against the counter.

"Ophelia said she can meet us in fifteen minutes. Can you be ready?"

"You bet."

As soon as she disconnected, Elana returned the flowers to the cooler. The excitement at soon banishing Kalan Murdoch from her mind wasn't zinging through her body as she expected. He'd been in her dreams each night for years. She'd miss him, but unfulfilled wishes were a drag.

Determined not to waffle any more than she already had, she grabbed her purse and left after locking up. Once she arrived at Izzy's old house, both her friend and some old woman in a long black dress she'd never seen before were waiting for her at the end of the path leading to Izzy's front door.

Elana parked, and kept her gaze on Ophelia. It was hard to believe the woman could even remember a spell at her age let alone do a successful one. Given her long white hair and skin thinner than onion paper, she had to be close to ninety.

When Elana slipped out of her Subaru, the sun was out in full force and the wind was sufficient enough to blow pollen around to perfume the air. Elana inhaled and the tension in her shoulders released.

As she neared, Ophelia seemed to look right through her. The small smile on her lips then disappeared. "Elana, something is troubling you."

Many things were, but the biggest was her obsession with Kalan. "I can't seem to get a particular man out of my head and it's affecting my sleep. It's clear he doesn't want to be with me, and I want to block his image, if that's possible."

"Most definitely, but I was sensing something else."

Her pulse soared. "What do you mean?"

She waved a hand. "It's nothing. Now tell me this man's name."

Surely, Izzy had told it to her. The old lady was losing it. "His name is Kalan Murdoch." Elana swore the old woman's eyes sparkled. Certainly, she wasn't under his sexual spell. Good Lord, the woman probably hadn't had sex in thirty years. "Do you know him?"

"Yes, my dear. I'm aware of most of our residents."

As much as Elana wanted to learn what the witch thought of him, she was here to banish him from her thoughts, not enhance them. "So what do I have to do?" *Cut up flowers and mash them? Dunk my head in a bowl of water for thirty seconds?* Clearly, spells were not her thing.

Ophelia smiled, and Elana could see the woman had been a beauty in her day. "Give me your hands."

That seemed simple enough. Ophelia closed her eyes and when her body shook, Elana worried the woman might be having a stroke. She then began to chant, though Elana had no idea what she was saying. The pressure on her fingers increased, as if the witch was squeezing out Kalan's image. The stronger her grip, the freer Elana began to feel.

Ophelia suddenly let go and smiled. "The next time you see your man, things will have changed. With him not clouding your thoughts, your true beauty will shine through."

"Thank you." Though she wasn't quite sure what that meant.

Before she could pay the woman or ask her more questions, the witch in the long gauzy dress spun around and disappeared behind the house, her hair flowing in the wind. Elana glanced at Izzy.

Her friend rushed up to her. "Do you feel any different?"

"I don't know, but I think I'm lighter."

"That's because you no longer have to worry about Kalan."

Elana should be thrilled, but because he had been part of her life for so long, she missed him already. "I didn't have the chance to pay her."

Izzy smiled. "Witches don't accept payment. At least the Wendayan witches don't."

"Okay, then. I guess that's done." She clenched her fists. "Did she say how long this spell lasts? I'd hate to think I was cured and then have a relapse."

Izzy wrapped an arm around her shoulder. "I didn't ask her, but I'm thinking it was a complete exorcism."

Her chest sunk in. "Good." Izzy probably wanted to get back to Rye. "Thank you for finding Ophelia."

"Anytime."

BRIAN STANLEY WAS on a mission. He needed to find his parents and his baby sister, though he suspected she didn't even know he existed. More than likely, she'd been as emotionally abused as he'd been, but that didn't mean she would be an ally.

He might have been born in Silver Lake, but he wasn't quite sure of the family's address, just that the estate was on the west side of town. After twenty-seven years, things had changed. That was why he'd gone to a bar, hoping someone could help him. The outside of McKinnon's Pub and Pool looked clean and in good repair, which meant Brian probably wouldn't end up in some stupid ass brawl or in a ditch out back.

"What can I get you?" the bartender asked. The man's nametag read Finn, and he looked like an affable young man.

"A shot of whiskey, Finn." Brian was still on his meds and probably shouldn't drink, but he'd dreamed of this moment for many years—or maybe it was more that he'd dreaded it.

"Here ya go. Want to run a tab?" Finn had given him a healthy dose of scotch. No skimping from this fellow.

It was tempting, but he had a lot to learn and didn't need his brain muddled. "No thanks."

Extracting his wallet, he slapped a twenty on the counter. While he had a credit card, flashing his name around wouldn't have been smart, since he had no idea how well known his parents were. Given what he'd read up on them, they were quite wealthy, implying many in this small town might know them. Brian could certainly use a family handout right about now, but that wasn't why he'd come.

Finn slipped the money off the counter and returned with change. "Let me know if you need anything else."

"There is one thing." His damn hand shook. Stupid meds. While he'd rehearsed what he planned to ask for years, now that he was back in town, he was losing his courage. "I'm just passing through, but I once did business with a Richard Stanley. I believe he said he was from Silver Lake."

"He is, but I've never met the man. He lives in the big white house on the corner of Langston and Pine."

Brian didn't want to act too knowledgeable about the area. "Where's that?"

"If you head west on Maple and hang a left on Pine View, you'll hit Pine Avenue. Can't miss the house."

"Thanks." He remembered there were two streets named Pine. While he didn't have the street number, he'd ask the cab driver to drop him off nearby. He'd find it. Brian tossed back his drink then retrieved all but a few bucks for a tip. As if he had all the time in the world, he slid off his stool and sauntered out.

Despite all the years of therapy, he wasn't sure how he wanted to handle meeting the *folks*. To be honest, he doubted they'd even recognize their son. The last time he'd seen them he was eight. His hair had been lighter and he'd been skinny. Now he could stand to shed a few pounds.

According to the mental hospital, his parents had called to check on his progress, but they'd never driven the six hours north to actually see him. All they'd wanted to know was if he was still killing animals and setting fires. The answer had been no, though recently, he'd been tempted. His abandonment issues were what had caused him to lash out, but apparently, they hadn't cared to read the telltale signs.

Fifteen minutes after calling a cab, his ride arrived. Instead of having the man drive him to the exact corner, he asked to be dropped off about a half mile away. He wasn't sure why he needed the precaution, but his common sense had clicked in.

By the time he arrived at the house where he'd grown up, it was too dark to tell the condition of the place, but the trees sure as hell were taller. Tonight, his plan was merely to case the joint. The confrontation would happen later when he was more emotionally prepared for the fallout.

The road was fairly secluded and the homes were spaced far apart, which made it perfect for surveillance. The lights were on in the house, but it didn't mean his parents were home. They could be having dinner out. From what he'd been able to tell, they'd been out of the country for some time, but from his mom's Facebook posts to her friends, they'd recently returned. Wouldn't she freak out if she knew he'd been pretending to be Harriett Longworth, an old time high school friend, in order to be accepted as her friend? If his mother had really cared about Harriett, she'd have known her old buddy was dead.

He ducked down the driveway then walked behind the line of trees, not wanting the lights from the house to cast any shadows. Close to the halfway point, headlights turned down the driveway. His heart racing, he plastered his back against a tree. When the car drove by, he dared to check it out. It was light colored and small, but he was unable to be certain of the model. He'd get a closer look once the occupant was inside.

A rather short woman emerged from the car, her hair pulled back in a ponytail. Certainly wasn't his mother. She was tall—or at least she had been to an eight year old. At this hour, it wouldn't be any of the staff. It might be a lawyer or even their accountant, summoned to their home.

When the woman rang the bell, he deleted his mom from the list. Needing to see and hear better, he crept closer to the house. The leaves had yet to fall, making it relatively easy to move about quietly. As long as his parents didn't have an outside dog, he'd be safe.

The woman was ushered inside and he slid to the side of the house where he could peek in the window that was part of the dining room but which opened into the living room. When he looked in, his stomach churned, his head swam, and bile rose up his throat. His parents were in the hallway speaking with the woman who looked rather young. As if she'd seen him, she turned her head in his general direction, and at that very moment, he was positive that he was looking into the face of his baby sister.

Chapter Four

KALAN TOOK HIS usual seat on the lounge chair at Rye's house, keeping an eye on Izzy baking cookies a few feet away. "Those chocolate chip you making?" Kalan asked, his stomach grumbling. They were his favorites.

"Yup. They smell good, don't they?" She smiled, but he refused to be sentimental at the domestic scene.

"Mouth-watering." When he was about eleven or twelve, he'd woken up early one morning to the stench of smoke and charred ashes.

"What are you grinning about?" Rye asked.

He waved a hand. "Just remembering when Blair was about six, she decided to make some cookies before our parents woke up."

"I take it they weren't edible."

He shook his head. "Let's say the smoke alarms went off, and the cookie sheets had to be thrown out. Blair must have cried for hours."

Rye chuckled. "Remind me not to accept any dinner invitations from your sister."

"Amen."

Izzy came into the living room and placed a small plate of cookies in front of him and another in front of Rye. "Thought you could use some of these given all the hard work the two of you are doing." She winked.

"We're about to start," Kalan said stuffing the wonderful smelling dessert in his mouth. "Oh, these are fucking good."

"It's a special recipe I learned when I was in France."

He glanced over at Rye. *"You lucky dog. She's hot and she cooks?"* he telepathed.

Rye just grinned. Kalan snatched another cookie. He didn't remember anything tasting this amazing since before his granny died. "Did you put red wine in these?" He ran his tongue along the roof of his mouth, attempting to detect what was different about them.

"Why would I put wine in cookies?" Her scrunched up nose implied she found the idea rather unpleasant. Little did she know.

"My dad's mom used to bake the best chocolate chip cookies. After she passed, we found her recipe box. Her secret?"

"Red wine?"

"You guessed it."

"You'll have to be satisfied with my unadorned ones." Izzy smiled and headed back into the open kitchen.

With the recipe exchange finished, Rye cleared his throat. "Are you thinking a Changeling is responsible for the Donaldson fire?"

It was what he'd been working on all day yesterday and today. Kalan didn't often discuss police business with Rye, except when it might involve other shifters—both good and bad. "We have no leads as of yet. I have it from three witnesses who say Jack Donaldson was at a church social during the time of the blaze, but a new witness said he was very sure he'd spotted him at the hardware store around the same time."

"It was a red moon. Could it have been a Changeling clone to throw suspicion his way?"

"Possibly."

"Even though a shifter might be involved, I'll let your department worry about it," Rye said. "If you learn anything concrete, I'll help."

"I'll keep you in the loop."

Izzy came out of the kitchen wiping her hands on a towel. "I saw you and Elana talking at my party. How did that go?"

His insides tightened. Clearly, she was on a fishing expedition since Elana was her best friend. He had no doubt they'd spoken about his less than friendly actions. If he could change things he would, but it was as if something had invaded his body and turned him into a bumbling bear. "Fine, I guess."

"She's been my friend since grade school, you know."

His stomach flipped, awaiting the speech about him being a jerk to her. He didn't need to be having this conversation. Thankfully, hearing Elana's name wasn't causing any internal changes. "That's nice."

Izzy dropped down next to Rye and picked up a cookie from her mate's pile. "Just so you know, she had a rough childhood and spent a lot of time with my family."

Kill me now. He didn't need to learn this, and he definitely didn't need to be engaging in this conversation. "That's a shame."

"Did you know her parents were out of the country for much of the time when she was growing up and left her alone with different housekeepers?"

Abandoning children really pissed him off. "Why have kids if you aren't going to enjoy them and nurture them?"

"Exactly. Being of British descent, my family was admittedly rather prim and proper, but they loved Missy and me totally and completely. They were always there for us."

He couldn't begin to imagine what it would be like not to have his parents and siblings around. "Me too. Does she have any brothers or sisters?"

"No, which was why she practically lived with us. Elana and I were in the same class together."

That put the scrumptious woman even further off limits, which might be a good thing. Kalan wasn't good with long term anything—except being Beta to his Silver Lake *Were* Clan. "I hope she's been able to work things out with her parents now that she's grown."

"Not really, which is why she stays away from them as much as possible. When they are back in town, they might do birthdays and holidays, but that's it."

Kalan tried to dismiss the ideas of being *alone, abandoned, and unloved*, but the pain from her upbringing altered something inside him. He swung his legs off the lounge. "I need to be going."

"Already? You two haven't done much work."

"Izzy," Rye said. "Let the poor man be."

Rye couldn't know how he felt about Elana, and he didn't intend to tell him.

"Before you leave," Izzy said, "I'll make a care package of cookies for you."

"You don't have to do that." He was surprised she wanted to, given she seemed to believe he'd mistreated her best friend.

"I know, but I want to. Give me a sec."

She stepped behind the kitchen island and returned with a large tin. She slid the cookies he hadn't eaten in there too. "Don't eat all of them at once. Spread them out over a few days."

He chuckled, never having witnessed this whimsical side of Izzy before. "You sound like my mom."

"I hope that's a good thing."

"It is." With tin in hand, he left. Tonight might be a good time for a run. Lumbering around in his bear form would help clear his head and help wear off the calories from those delicious cookies.

BRIAN HAD WAITED two long days before confronting his parents. What he expected them to say he didn't know, but he steeled himself for their continued rejection. An apology would be too good to be true, but even if he received one, it couldn't make up for the twenty-seven years of being in and out of mental institutions. His suffering over how they'd treated him had fucked with his head really bad.

The cab dropped him off at the house. This time he didn't care if there was a log of his arrival. Because it was still light, he studied the home and the long driveway, which was bordered by maples and oaks that led to the huge white mansion with green shutters. He couldn't help but look at the window where his room had been and to the roof access where he would often climb out at night. Seeing the old homestead was like a hundred knives stabbing his gut, but he refused to turn back now.

I can do this. I just need to put one foot in front of the other. His therapist thought this would be a good idea, saying Brian would never have closure unless he spoke with them. Now that the time was here, he doubted the wisdom of that decision.

At the front door, his hand shook as he raised it and knocked. They hadn't even changed the lion's head brass knocker or the color of the red door from when he lived there. Heart clamoring to escape, he lifted his elbows to keep his underarms from sweating.

The front door opened.

It was his mom, and a band around his chest threatened to cut off his air. She looked old. She might have dyed her hair blonde to halt the aging process, but he'd know her anywhere. She had the same beady eyes, long nose, and stern mouth.

"Yes?" she said in that haughty voice he detested.

"Hello, Mother." At least that came out sounding almost normal.

She stilled, but the pulse in her neck did a rapid tattoo. Taking a few steps back, she placed her hand on the banister and called to someone upstairs. "Can you come down here, please?"

Holy shit. His fucking mother was actually scared of him. That put things in a different light. "May I come in?"

"Just one moment."

Footsteps sounded on the stairs, or rather footsteps along with a thump of a cane. When a gray-headed man appeared, Brian didn't recognize his father at first, but then the eyes gave him away. He'd always stood so ramrod straight, and now he was a gimp with slumped shoulders.

Dad moved next to Mom, presenting a united front. "May we help you?" his father asked.

"Richard, this is Brian, our son, or so he claims."

Did she call him by name because his father didn't remember?

Unless he had a form of dementia, it reinforced just what kind of lame people they were.

"Do you have proof you're our Brian?" his father asked.

The word *our* softened him. Maybe his dad had changed. "Look at me. I have your blue eyes and mom's long nose." He would have rolled up his sleeves to show the massive scarring from all the intravenous drugs they'd administered over the years, but they'd say he was some kind of drug addict. "Surely, you remember that you sent away your eight-year old son to the loony bin, because you were afraid I'd burn down the house or kill you."

"Nonsense," his mother said, her gaze looking everywhere but at him. "We were afraid you'd hurt yourself."

That was a lie. "After years of therapy, I've been declared sane. I don't set things on fire or harm animals either."

"That's good to hear. Do you want to come in?" The strain in her voice sounded like fingernails on a chalkboard.

Her invitation took long enough, though now he wasn't sure he wanted to spend any time with these monsters. After wiping his feet just as he'd been taught to do as a young boy, he entered, interested to learn what things they'd kept and what they'd changed. "I see the picture of Blue Boy over the fireplace is the same, but thankfully you got rid of those godawful flowered sofas."

His mother sucked in a breath, but he didn't miss the evil shooting from her eyes. "Brian, we're sorry that we sent you away, but once the baby arrived, we thought you'd harm her."

Sorry, my ass. That excuse was even lamer. "She didn't interest me."

His father moved back. "Let's sit in the living room and you can catch us up."

Now his father was interested in what he had to say? By asking him to sit, Dad must believe he needed Brian to calm down, that he'd come to harm them, or perhaps blackmail them for money. While the idea of asking for money had merit, Brian just wanted an apology, but he suspected he'd have to wait a very long time for one.

Too bad, he had no intention of being in Silver Lake longer than necessary.

"Can I bring you some tea?" his mom asked, acting as if this visit was an everyday occurrence.

"How about a beer?" He wasn't eight any more.

She glanced at his father who imperceptibly nodded. "I'll get one for you."

His father limped over to a striped high-back chair and dropped down. "Tell us why you've come."

Now the cold, unfeeling son of a bitch father he remembered surfaced. "I guess I needed to hear from your own lips why you sent me away and why you never visited me."

His mom returned through a door carrying a beer and handed it to him. "I'll answer that. Your therapist forbade us to. We tried to see you, but he thought it would slow your healing if we spoke."

Brian chugged back the brew, helping to quench his thirst. He didn't believe a word of it. In retrospect, it was probably for the best. They weren't sorry that they'd ditched their kid. "Well, thank you for that." Surely, they'd hear the sarcasm in his voice.

"Brian, you need to understand. We didn't want to do it," his father said, sounding pathetic.

"Too late now." African masks hung on the far wall, and a statue of the Eiffel Tower along with what looked like a green onyx pyramid sat on the coffee table. "I see you've traveled a lot."

Once more, their wide eyes gave away their fear. "You know what we do for a living. Travel is necessary."

Given the size of the house, the expensive rugs on the floor, and the paintings that he bet were originals, they could have hired someone to shop for them. "Eight months out of the year?"

"Yes," his mother said, lifting her chin in defiance.

Brian wanted to hurt them like they'd hurt him. He stood. "I gotta take a leak."

"It's down the—"

"I remember where it is."

Brian set his bottle on an expensive looking mahogany table not caring if he left a ring, and headed down the hallway past the kitchen to the small half bath. He didn't have to go. He just needed to get away from them for a while, to have a chance to think.

Once he was out of their sight, he paced. Before he was able to come up with a plan, the front doorbell rang. Company. Good. That gave him a good excuse to leave and regroup. To his surprise, loud shouts came from the living room. Maybe the Feds were there to arrest them for doing something illegal—like not paying taxes. Wouldn't that be sweet?

Brian stepped back into the living room and stopped in his tracks. Three sets of eyes shot to him and he swore they could see right through him. These were no Feds. All three were dressed in slogan T-shirts and ripped jeans, and the men varied in height and age.

His mother piped up. "This is my son, Brian. He's just passing through town."

Brian took a few steps, not because he wanted to be nearer to these fellows, but because he'd be closer to the front door in case something bad went down.

The big, tall fellow stepped forward and shook his hand. "Nice to meet you." He then turned to his dad. "Forty-eight hours."

His father smiled. "No problem. It'll be here."

It? Before Brian could say he wanted to leave, the three amigos left. He turned to his parents, a bit confused about what he'd witnessed. "What was that about?"

The father waved a hand. "We've been having trouble getting something they'd ordered from India, but it'll be here in two days. Nothing to worry about."

Brian nodded. "I need to head back to town."

"Do you want to stay here?" his mother said. From the bitter tone, she wanted him to say no.

"I've already paid for a place in town. I don't plan to be here long."

Her lips pinched. "Elana is coming over this weekend. Maybe you'd like to see your little sister. She's all grown up."

"Sure." Or not. His head was spinning with too much emotion and he was losing control. "Talk to you later."

He rushed out, relishing the long walk back to town.

Chapter Five

After working late at the station, Kalan had dropped into bed, and seven hours later he'd woken up refreshed. For the first time since he'd seen Elana at the hospital, he'd actually had a full night sleep—no raging hard-on or erotic dreams starring the pretty lady.

Stretching, he patted his gut to make sure he hadn't grown a second stomach overnight. He hadn't eaten that many cookies in a long time. It was all Izzy's fault for making them so damned good. She deserved some kind of medal for that recipe. It was almost as if the added sugar had set him back on track.

Kalan slid out of bed, cleaned up, and dressed in a ratty T-shirt and shorts. It was his day off, and he was determined to enjoy it. The run last night had done wonders for his attitude—or else it had been the cookies.

After hours of thinking, he'd finally figured out that the stress of taking over for his father must have affected him more than he'd realized. A kind of calmness had enveloped him, so much that he believed he would be capable of acting his usual self around Elana—self-confident, charming, and dare he say macho.

He whipped up some breakfast then stacked the dirty dishes in the dishwasher. Kalan liked order, but was willing to wing it when it came to women, loving nothing more than to make them happy.

Thinking of women, his thoughts returned to Elana yet again. Sympathy swamped him at what she'd had to endure growing up, and then pride swelled at how she'd overcome adversity to create something as wonderful as her flower shop. A young woman opening a business in today's economy would have run against some pretty hefty odds, yet Elana had flourished. Or should he say, blossomed?

He shook his head at the way he'd acted around her all three times. Now he knew it had all been due to stress. Seeing things clearly for the first time in days, he realized a woman like Elana deserved happiness. While he had no intention of being with her on a steady basis, he bet she'd appreciate it if he took her to lunch. They'd chat about Izzy and how happy she was, and then he'd steer the conversation to her shop. He bet she could talk for days about what it entailed to be a successful entrepreneur.

At his excellent idea, a sense of generosity rose inside him. Taking her to the Silver Lake café or to Nate's Pizzeria would be too ordinary. He wanted something special—something she'd remember. He snapped his fingers. He bet she'd like a picnic. The weather would be turning cooler soon and he bet she'd appreciate taking advantage of the balmy conditions while they lasted.

The question was where to go for this outdoor adventure? She didn't know he was a shifter, so that nixed the area around Silver Lake. A nice mountain view would be spectacular, but most of the areas overlooking the Smoky Mountains required a hike, and she probably didn't have a lot of time during her lunch break. From what Izzy had told him, she was devoted to her job.

Mentally scanning what the town had to offer, he landed on the region across from the church. The town had put in a real nice park that included picnic shelters. Families with small children would be there, making the experience upbeat and pleasant. Perfect. That solved one dilemma.

Since he'd be bringing the food, all he needed was to find out what Elana liked to eat. Once, many moons ago, he and a date had gone on a hike. Needing something for lunch, he'd packed peanut butter and jelly sandwiches only to find out she was allergic to peanuts. He wouldn't make that mistake again. If Izzy wasn't home, he'd stop at the Crystal Winds Spa and ask her what Elana enjoyed.

Maybe he'd even buy her a present, and say it was because he'd been out of sorts for the last few weeks, and that he normally didn't act like a bumbling idiot around women. Flowers were out of the question, but from experience, he found women always liked chocolate. Coming prepared to a date would let her know he was a nice guy. Going out with her would also convince him that his intense attraction and desire had been a fluke.

Because lunch wouldn't be for another few hours, he straightened up his house then read over the Donaldson file to see if he'd missed anything. Around eleven, he drove to town. Elana most likely wouldn't recognize his Jeep, so he parked in front of the Crystal Winds Spa and dashed inside. He hadn't stepped foot in the place in several years, but the store hadn't changed much other than the beauty and health products that were on the shelves appeared new.

Izzy rushed toward him. "Is Rye okay?"

Crap. It hadn't occurred to him she might draw that conclusion. "He's fine. I'm here because I wanted to ask you something about Elana."

Her eyes shone. "Really? What is it?"

"I wanted to do something nice for her and thought she might appreciate a picnic lunch."

Izzy cocked a brow. "Why the sudden change of heart?"

No way could he tell her that he finally realized that stress had caused his body to go crazy around Elana. "After hearing how she'd grown up, I thought she'd appreciate the gesture. Is that a crime?"

"No, but she'll spot a pity date in a heartbeat. She'll think I put you up to it."

Fuck. "You didn't."

"I know that, but she won't."

The air rushed out of his lungs. "What do you suggest? To be honest, I feel bad about the way I've acted around her lately."

Izzy lifted a shoulder. "Then tell her that. Just don't mention you heard about how her parents had mistreated her."

"I promise." He held up three fingers as if he was back in Boy Scouts. He also didn't want to lead her on. Damn. This might not be a good idea.

For a few minutes they batted around lunch suggestions, until he was satisfied he had the perfect meal. Armed with a list of what things Elana liked and didn't like, he headed over to the U-Save supermarket where he purchased fried chicken, potato salad, baked beans, and a small box of chocolate. Because he wasn't allowed to take alcohol to the park, he picked up some bottled water. Hopefully, she'd understand this was a spur of the moment idea, which made something fancy and elaborate not possible.

Leaving the food in the back of his Jeep, he parked in front of her store and headed on in. To his total dismay, he took one look at Elana in a pretty pink dress, and his body went haywire. What the fuck? He thought he'd been cured.

"Kalan. What are you doing here?" She pushed some wisps of hair back from her face then redid her ponytail as if it mattered what she looked like.

He couldn't tell if she was delighted, frightened, or dismayed. From behind his back, he placed the small box of chocolate on the counter. "I came to apologize."

A burst of excitement shot through him that he was no longer stumbling and fumbling.

Her hands stilled as if she thought this was some kind of trick. "Apologize for what?"

Shit. He certainly couldn't say his inner bear was constantly trying to get out every time he was near her. "I've been under a lot of stress lately, and I wasn't as attentive to you at the party as I'd wanted."

Her eyes shone brighter than the sun. "You didn't have to buy me anything. I understand what stress can do to a person."

Her comment was more proof that he had been a jerk, but he didn't need to list all of his mistakes. "Listen, I picked up a few things for a picnic. I know you can't leave the store for long, but I was wondering if you'd be willing to take a lunch break at the park?" Sounds from the back indicated she had help.

Her cheeks flushed a delicate rose color, and her blue eyes seemed to turn a darker shade of cobalt. "I'd love to. Let me tell my assistant."

Elana practically ran to the back, indicating she was excited and not dismayed. So far, so good. He figured once they ate a nice lunch and chatted, the guilt over how he'd acted would surely go away. If his bear would stop being such a demanding ass, he'd call this idea a total success.

At one point, Kalan had been tempted to find a willing female to help get his rocks off, but there was something about the way he reacted to Elana that told him no one else would satisfy him—or could satisfy him. *Damn.* Taking her out only to have his way with her, though, would get her hopes up, and then he couldn't abandon her. If he did, he'd be no better than her parents. No question about it. He had to keep his dick in his pants.

"I'm ready," she said.

She'd reapplied her lipstick and blush. The woman seemed to be trying to lure him, but he couldn't let her succeed, but damn that fresh rose scent of her had his bear pushing and growling.

Due to her time constraint, he drove them to the park just a few blocks away instead of suggesting they walk. After finding a parking space, he carried the bag of groceries to a table close to where the kids were playing. "This okay?"

Her quick broad smile sent a surge of delight straight through him. "Absolutely."

"I hope you like fried chicken."

Her bow-shaped mouth reopened. "It's my favorite."

Thank you, Izzy. She hadn't steered him wrong.

The table was near to where several toddlers were running around, and Elana's look of longing piqued his interest. "Those kids sure are cute, aren't they? You ever dream of a few of your own?"

She shook her head. "I'm not sure I want any. I'm so busy running my store that I wouldn't know how to care for them when I'm at work."

He should have thought of that. She wouldn't want to repeat the mistakes of her parents. While he didn't want to rub it in her face that his parents were always around for him and his siblings, she might think it odd if he didn't say something about his upbringing. "My mom was lucky that she could stay home and take care of the kids while Dad worked." He set the bag on the table.

"I might be in the minority, but I like working."

That intrigued him. If he had infinite funds, he probably would still work for the sheriff's department. "I'm like you. I couldn't sit home and not help others, but my mom worked hard taking care of us. We were quite a handful." Shifting, breaking things, and causing a lot of trouble. He placed the container of potato salad on the table along with the baked beans. "I didn't know what you liked to drink, so I picked up some bottled water."

"Water's fine." She grabbed the drink, opened it, and took a swig. "I know Blair and your brother Jackson because we were in school together, but do you have any other siblings?"

"No. I think the three of us were enough to handle." That was an understatement.

Elana sat across from him on the wooden bench and picked up a paper plate. With care, she scooped the beans and potato salad onto it. "What made you go into law enforcement?" she asked.

That was an easy one to answer. "Being six-three and a bit large, I was always called on to break up fights. Since my father used to be in the security business, I kind of fell into the whole protecting others thing. I could have worked for McKinnon and Associates, but I wanted to do something different."

When she bit into her chicken, her moan caused his libido to shoot into high gear again. Kalan looked above her head to the children at play, hoping to gain some control. If nothing else, he wanted to figure out what it was about Elana that always had his cock at attention.

"Aren't you afraid you'll get hurt or killed?"

Her comment cut short his distraction. Now would be the perfect time to tell her he was a shifter, that he healed quickly, and that he was stronger than a human, only it wouldn't serve any purpose. She might not have blabbed to the world that Izzy's mate was a werewolf, or that Izzy now was one too, but why chance a leak?

"There's always that risk."

She swiped a napkin across her luscious lips and his thoughts rocketed to what it would be like to kiss her. *Stop it.* He might be able to have a coherent conversation with her now, and actually enjoy it, but his inner animal was not willing to cooperate.

"What was your most exciting case?" Elana rested her elbows on the table and leaned forward.

The wind brushed back her rather out of control hair, and she couldn't have been prettier. A hint of honeysuckle tinged the air, making this a perfect day. Thankfully, the pink shirtwaist dress she'd worn covered her tits. If he'd even had a glimpse of her cleavage, he might have had to excuse himself.

She asked you a question, dickweed. "Exciting? That might not apply to any of my cases, but perhaps my most *rewarding* one involved locating a kidnapper."

"Can you tell me about it? I'll understand if it needs to stay hushed up."

Hushed up? Cute. "The case is closed now, so I can tell you a little about it. We were able to use the GPS signal from the fugitive's cell to find him. For days, he'd been so careful, but for some reason, that day he turned it on, allowing us to find his general location. Add in an eye witness, and we were able to locate the little girl unharmed."

"Wow. That was wonderful, but I bet you've experienced heartache too."

Many people never consider the toll this job had on a cop, but Elana seemed to possess a lot of empathy. It was almost as if she were a witch herself. "Yes, quite a lot, but the people involved always suffer more." He didn't want to spend their *date* talking about him though. "Enough about me. How did you get started in the flower business?"

She helped herself to more beans and another piece of fried chicken. "Growing up, we had a gardener who was really nice to me. We also had a cook, but she didn't like me hanging out in the kitchen, which is why I suck at cooking, despite my large size."

Her comment about her size dug a hole in him. "I love your body." *Oh, fuck.* He hadn't meant to blurt that out.

Her lips pressed together. "You don't have to be nice just because I'm Izzy's friend."

Being unjustly accused of something really got his goat. "Izzy has nothing to do with this." That was as much as he was willing to say about the matter. No way would he tell her that because he was a larger man, he liked a woman he didn't feel he'd crush if they were in bed.

"Oh, sorry." Her face colored an appealing shade of pink. "Anyway, I spent a lot of time outdoors watching our gardener, Mr. Jenkins, take care of the plants. His wife helped out in the spring, planting the flowers, and she'd taken the time to explain things, like what plants grew well and how to take care of them."

As lovely as that story was, his heart ached as he pictured her as a little girl not having her mom to teach her those things. "Starting a business takes a lot of work, but also cash."

If her parents had lent her the start-up money, they couldn't be all bad.

"Don't I know it? Izzy's dad was nice enough to lend me the money, which I'm paying back every month. Not only does he own the cellular phone store and the entire strip mall, he owns my building across the street too."

Rye had mentioned that a while back. So much for nice parents, but if they raised such a wonderful daughter, they had to have some redeeming qualities. "I bet your parents are proud of what you've accomplished." He had to act as if he knew nothing.

"They haven't really said. I do know they're happy I didn't want to go into their import-export business with them."

Don't even go there. Kalan's body shot into protective mode, and that meant it wanted to shift. He inhaled deeply to forestall that event. "Well, I think you're remarkable."

If her parents were too self-centered to care, it was their loss.

Her face turned a slightly darker shade of pink this time. Damn. He'd never met a woman who seemed unaware of how amazing she was. Kalan wasn't going to let her work ethic, coupled with her lack of ego, get to him though. He didn't want a steady girlfriend—not with taking over the Clan business.

"Thank you, but I think you're pretty remarkable too."

For some reason, her comment took him aback. Had she been aware he was a bear shifter, he might have understood her sentiment. A human would be impressed he could alter his form, but she was only commenting about who he was as a man, and that pleased him. "I appreciate you saying that."

Her eyes widened. "I'm sure you were told how wonderful you were your whole life."

"My parents loved us kids more than life itself and wanted us to be the best we could be, but at times they were hard yet nurturing. They really believed in personal responsibility. That's my way of saying, I wasn't always praised at every turn."

As if she was uncomfortable with his comment, she delved into her potato salad. When she finished, she looked up at him. "I think by taking the time to teach you the difference between right and wrong, it was their way of telling you how wonderful you were."

Her profound words really hit home. "You might be right. You seemed to have learned how to be successful and a nice person despite your folks not being around." From what she told him today, it was reasonable to draw that conclusion.

"I had a good support system." She looked off to the side as she finished the food on her plate. "I probably should be getting back to work."

Elana stood, gathered the trash and dumped it in a garbage can while Kalan just sat there, a bit stunned. No woman had ever cut short a date, especially after he'd just complimented her. His ego wasn't used to the beating. "Is something wrong?"

Elana returned. "No. Lunch was wonderful. Thank you, but I do have a store to run."

Was her flower shop so busy that she couldn't take a full hour for lunch? "I'll drive you back."

He escorted her to his Jeep, happy he'd recently washed and cleaned it. With her sudden dismissal of their date, however, he was unsure what to say to make things better between them. He slipped in his side and started the engine. "Maybe we can do this again."

Never in his wildest dream did he think he'd ask her for a second date, but she'd gotten under his skin.

Thankfully, her smile implied he'd said the right thing. "I'd like that."

That was easier than he expected. Kalan drove slowly, hoping to prolong their time together. "What kind of things do you like to do when you're not running your store?"

She glanced out the window. "I read a lot."

Reading wasn't exactly something they could do together as it cut out the talking part—and the kissing too. Of course, if she read him some sexy scenes, it might get them in the mood. Before he could ask what she liked to read, they'd arrived. He parked in front, rushed over to her side, and held open the door. "Do you like to go to the movies?"

Elana faced him, shielding her eyes from the sun. "Yes, but I don't see you as the romantic comedy type, which is about all I ever see."

No, he liked the action adventure movies, but he could sit through anything. "You don't think I like romance?"

Shit. Him and his big mouth.

The wind picked up, whipping a few strands out of her elastic. He wanted to brush it behind her ears, but he didn't dare touch her.

She shrugged. "You seem more of the rough and tumble type. I can picture you riding a motorcycle, jumping out of planes, and maybe even doing some MMA fighting."

He cracked up. "I see I have my work cut out for me, showing you the real me." Goddess in heaven, he couldn't believe he'd just said that. What was happening to him? It was as if someone else had possessed his body. Damn bear. "I used to own a motorcycle, and I have done some skydiving, but I've never taken any martial arts classes." Mostly because he could shift and beat any attacker. "Do you like to ski?"

She laughed. "It's a little too warm for that."

Crap. Nothing was coming out right. "I meant in the winter."

Elana grinned then winked. "I know what you meant. No, I don't ski. I've always been a big girl. Exercising wasn't my forte."

"That's okay. We can just talk." *And kiss. And fuck. No, no, no.* He had to stop thinking with his cock.

She looked behind her as if she expected her assistant to be waving at her to come in. "Look, I really need to go. Thank you for the picnic. It was really sweet of you."

Sweet? Kalan Murdoch didn't do sweet. Well, fuck. What had started out as a way to pay her back for being a dick turned out to be something a lot different than he'd ever anticipated. Now that he wanted to be with her, Elana didn't seem as interested. Well, damn.

Chapter Six

ELANA WAS UP in her apartment dressed in a T-shirt and yoga pants with a glass of red wine in one hand and the phone in the other.

"So you just got up and announced the date was over?" Izzy said, practically shouting.

Elana giggled. "I can't believe I did that. I mean, here I've dreamed of going out on a date with Kalan like for forever, and then I acted as if I couldn't have cared less."

"Why?"

That was a good question. Part of the reason had been he'd touched on the subject of her upbringing. If he learned how her parents had treated her, she bet he'd run—fast. "I kind of thought it would intrigue him. I have to say the look of surprise on his face was priceless."

"It could work in your favor since I doubt many women have ever turned down Kalan Murdoch." Her tone turned more pensive.

She hadn't been totally truthful. "He suggested we go out again sometime, and I said yes. I tried not to sound too excited, but I'm not sure if I succeeded."

"That's great. You want him to think you're willing but not anxious. Wait a minute. I thought you wanted to erase him from your mind."

"I did, but that spell was clearly bogus. I don't think that old lady could make a voodoo doll work."

Izzy laughed. "Perhaps. So what happens now?"

"I wait and see if he calls. If not, there's no reason for me not to branch out. I made a few references to my larger-than-life frame, and he acted as if he liked my shape. Hell, if someone as hot and fit as Kalan appreciated my curves, perhaps others will too."

"Whoa. Who are you? Though I have to say I do like this new self-confidence."

It wouldn't do her any good. As soon as Kalan understood that she really was interested, he'd back off. "We'll see. So how are Rye's powers progressing?" As much as Elana wanted to ask if Izzy's were diminishing, as had been prophesized, it wouldn't be nice to bring up the sore subject.

Izzy laughed. "He's improving, but at the rate he's going, he'd have to live another five hundred years before he would have any real control over fire and wind. His water and earth skills are nil." Some noise sounded in the background. "That's Rye. He's home."

"I'll let you go. Thanks for chatting."

"Sure, hon, anytime."

A twinge of jealousy surfaced hearing the joy in her friend's voice. They'd always been in the same situation romantically their whole lives. Izzy avoided men because of her talents and Elana shied away from them mostly because she didn't want to be disappointed when they didn't return her affection.

This time, however, seemed different. Elana wasn't so bold as to believe that she would ever experience the full wonder of Kalan Murdoch. Spending an hour with him earlier this afternoon sure had helped make up for it though.

PHIL SMYTHE, KALAN'S boss, dodged between a few desks as he barreled toward him. The former military man always exuded a sense of power and control, but this time there seemed to be an added layer of seriousness along with a hint of shock.

"Kalan, we have one or possibly two homicides. According to the caller, a second victim is clinging to life. The ambulance is on their way there now." He placed an address on his desk. "Take Garner with you."

"Yes, sir." As adrenaline charged through him, Kalan pushed back his chair and headed off to find his partner. He didn't ask the identity of the victims. Too often, he knew them.

Because his thoughts had centered on Elana last night, he'd been lethargic all day from lack of sleep. Now that he was needed, the adrenaline was giving him a much-needed boost.

Dalton Garner entered the large room and rushed toward him, his gun strapped to his hip. Many of the staff liked to joke and call him Hollywood because of his classically good looks and amazingly thick hair, but at the moment, he appeared frazzled. "Phil just told me about the double homicide."

Silver Lake had their fair share of thefts and assaults, but rarely were people murdered—let alone two at one time.

"Hard to believe, but one might still be alive." Kalan glanced at the address, memorized it, and then handed it to Dalton.

In silence, they headed out to Kalan's cruiser, as he was the senior officer. Not that he'd dealt with many homicides in his ten years on the force, but Kalan had processed enough of them to know what to do. Out of habit, he glanced at the sky. It was clear and dark, with the white moon nearly full. Thank the goddess, it wasn't tinged with red.

Once under way, Dalton's fingers flew over the keyboard. "The owners on record are Richard and Gloria Stanley."

Kalan nearly veered off the road but righted his vehicle before going over the berm. "Shit."

"You know them?"

He racked his brain trying to remember if his boss had mentioned whether the victims were husband and wife. It was possible Elana had gone over to visit them and been murdered. His heart hammered in his chest so hard that he had to use his animal strength to keep control of the wheel. "I know their daughter."

"You just passed the turnoff."

Damn it. Working hard to focus, Kalan flipped on his sirens, turned right at the next street, and doubled back. When he neared the address, the flashing ambulance lights lit up the trees. He pulled in and then parked on the far side of the spacious drive, giving the paramedics room to maneuver.

"Let's do this," Kalan said, his stomach tied in knots. "*If you have any ability to grant a wish, Naliana, please don't let Elana be in there.*"

As they entered the grand house, the paramedics were waiting in the foyer. Kalan nodded to Jordan Ashworth. "What can you tell us?"

The coppery stench of blood assaulted him, but because of the mixture of different scents, he couldn't distinguish anything helpful. Another shifter had been there recently, but it didn't mean he was one of the killers.

"Both the wife and husband were dead when we arrived."

At the mention of the victims, relief poured in him. "What about the person who called it in?"

"We knocked, but when he didn't answer, we tested the front door and found it open, so we went in. The son's in there, in the same position as we found him. I immediately felt for signs of life but found none. Then we waited for you to arrive. We didn't move the bodies, but their son had his hands all over them."

The son? Kalan stepped to the side and stilled. His eyes were glazed over, and he was holding a knife. Blood stained the front of his shirt. Holy shit. "Thanks."

He and Dalton stepped into the large living room. Masks, paintings, and other artifacts that had graced the walls were now strewn on the floor. Sofas were ripped apart, drawers pulled out, and several more that appeared to be prized wall artifacts were on the floor, most of which were broken. *Shit*. It looked like a robbery gone wrong, but he wouldn't jump to any conclusions. Forensics would need to go over the place with care. Hopefully, they'd find some fingerprints or DNA.

Kalan nodded to Dalton. "Check for evidence of any other intruders and possible point of entry."

"I'm on it."

No other shifters were in the vicinity, so he was safe from them for now, but Kalan was unsure about the stability of the man holding the bloodied knife. He had shorn, dark hair and remained staring straight ahead, as if he wasn't even aware either of them had entered the room. As Kalan neared, he noticed the man's eyes were the same color as Elana's.

"You want to put the knife down, son?" It didn't matter that he looked to be about the same age as Kalan.

"I can't believe they're dead." His voice trailed off, but the depth of his grief didn't match the horror of the scene.

Kalan's hand hovered over his gun in case the man was amped up on drugs and charged him. "I'll ask you one more time. Put the knife down and move away from the body." Three seconds later, the man obeyed. "That's good. Now tell me your name."

"Brian Stanley."

So they did have a son, or else he was a nephew. "Want to tell me what happened, Brian?"

"I was coming over to talk to my folks, but when I got here, I found them on the floor, stabbed. My mother had a knife in her stomach but she was still breathing. I thought if I pulled it out, she might live." His brows pinched, clouded in confusion.

That was one of his many mistakes. "How about coming down to the station where we can sort this all out?"

Dalton returned and shook his head. Kalan stepped next to him and kept his voice low. "I'm going to take Brian in. Call for forensics to process the scene and wait here for them. I'll send someone for you when you're ready to return."

"Will do."

Kalan put on his purple crime scene gloves and helped Brian up. Because he couldn't be sure Brian wouldn't try to bolt, Dalton followed them out. Once at the cruiser, his partner helped by spreading a plastic sheet in back so as not to stain the seat.

"Where are you staying, Brian?" Kalan asked.

"At the Silver Lake Hotel." He narrowed his eyes. "I didn't kill them."

"I'm not accusing you of anything."

"Then why do I have to go to the police station?" His voice changed, and suddenly he sounded like a little kid.

"We need to take your statement."

Not needing to have a lengthy discussion in the drive when this man seemed a bit unstable, Kalan opened the back door to the cruiser and motioned for Brian to slide in. Fortunately, he entered without incident. The doors locked automatically, making any attempt to escape futile. Nothing about this crime was cut and dry. If it were a crime born out of anger, why stay around and wait for the cops? And why hadn't Elana mentioned she had a brother?

Even as Kalan radioed that he was bringing in the man who'd called in the murders, dread filled him at having to let Elana know that her parents were dead. It didn't matter that she didn't seem all that fond of them. It might be worse asking her where she was this evening, killing any chance she'd look at him the same way again. Bringing up the fact she had a brother might put a permanent wedge between them—assuming Brian Stanley was telling the truth.

He should have been relieved Elana might walk out of his life, but his protective side wasn't pleased.

Mate, mine.

He inwardly growled to shut his bear up.

Ten minutes later, Kalan parked in front of the sheriff's department and escorted Brian Stanley up the steps and into the main entrance. It might not be a full moon, but from the number of drunks, prostitutes, and other unsavory people waiting to be processed, it would be a long night.

Forensics would want to examine Brian's clothing for evidence, so he led him to a room near the back of the station and grabbed a set of maroon scrubs for him. "I'll need you to change into these.

Place your clothes in the bag on the table."

He held out his hands. "I'm bloody. Mind if I wash up at my hotel first? It's only a few blocks away."

"I'm sorry. We have rules."

As if he'd been told that line for years, his shoulders slumped as he shuffled into the room. Once the door was secure, Kalan returned to the front and asked for a forensic officer to check out Brian. "When you're finished processing him, I need to ask him some questions in interrogation room two."

"Yes, sir."

While Brian was being processed, Kalan wanted to touch base with his boss. He knocked on Phil's door then stepped into his office that was stacked with mounds of papers despite the department trying to handle things electronically. Smythe slipped off his glasses and sat up straighter. "What did you find out?"

"Not much other than the son was holding his mother with one arm and had a bloody knife in the other."

"Was he was the one who called it in?"

"Yes."

"Is he looking good for it?" Phil's voice came out strained.

"My gut instinct says no. The man seemed to be in shock and a bit disoriented. We'll know more once we receive the coroner's report and the lab results from Brian's clothes."

"Where's the son now?"

"He's changing. When he's finished, I'll ask him more questions."

Smythe leaned back in his chair, the lines on his face etched around his eyes and mouth heavier than usual. The man wasn't more than forty-five, but the job seemed to be taking a toll on him today. "They have a daughter—an Elana Stanley—who lives downtown." Phil slipped him yet another piece of paper. "Here's her address and number. Inform her about her parents' death and find out where she was tonight."

"Will do." Hearing her name had his gut clenching, but he saw no reason to mention that he knew her.

With a heavy heart at having to break the news to Elana, Kalan headed to Interrogation Room number 2 carrying an old-fashioned pad of paper. There was something comforting to a witness if he saw that plain yellow-ruled paper instead of a more sterile electronic tablet.

While he waited, Kalan jotted down some questions. A few minutes later, an officer escorted Brian into the room wearing the borrowed scrubs.

"You want something to drink?" the officer asked Brian.

"Water's good." Brian's tone bordered on belligerence.

"Have a seat, Brian. I know your sister Elana, and I have to say I'm confused."

He pressed his lips together and rocked. "She doesn't know about me."

That answered one of his questions, though he found it difficult to reconcile, unless he was from another marriage. "Want to start from the beginning?"

Brian shifted in his seat and tugged on the V-neck top. "You won't believe me."

"Try me. If what you say is the truth, it should be easy to confirm."

He finally made eye contact. "Do I need a lawyer?"

Kalan was wondering when he'd ask. "If you think you need one. Do you?"

"I'm not sure." He rubbed his wrist. From the tan mark, he was used to wearing a watch.

Kalan checked his phone. "It's seven-thirty, if that's what you need to know."

"I need to take my meds soon."

Kalan made a note. "What kind of meds?"

"They're for my anxiety."

From the way Brian was having a hard time looking Kalan in the eye and shifting in his seat, he needed more than that. "Why doesn't

Elana know you exist?"

The answer to this question was probably only important to him.

"My parents sent me to a mental hospital right after she was born. They might not have told her about me. I don't know."

Brian was right. This wasn't looking good for him. "So she never visited?" Elana was such a caring soul. If she'd known about Brian, she would have.

"No. When I spoke with my parents the other day, they said they wanted to visit me, but that my therapist thought my healing would be set back if they did." He lowered his gaze. "Total bullshit. They just didn't want me."

He made a note that Brian had a hard time directly answering questions. If what he claimed were true, why have another child? Kalan hoped Elana might be able to shed some light on the situation, assuming she knew of her brother's existence. "You said you spoke with your parents before tonight?"

If that were true, why didn't he try to contact Elana as well? In retrospect, it was probably for the best. This man had some serious issues.

He explained how he went up to their door two days ago and had to convince them that he was their son.

"Did they finally believe you?"

"Eventually. I knew too much about the house since I lived there until I was eight."

Kalan would have to ask his dad if he remembered if the Stanleys had a son. Most likely, his father had no cause to interact with them, especially if they were out of town most of the time.

"Why did you return to the house if your folks didn't greet you with open arms the other day?"

Brian rubbed his hands together and stared at the pencil in Kalan's hand. "I didn't get to speak with them for more than a few minutes before company arrived. I was angry and hurt so I left."

That made sense. "What time did you arrive at your parents'

house this evening?"

"About fifteen minutes before you showed up."

Kalan scribbled the time on his pad then leaned back in his seat. "How did you get in if they'd both been stabbed?" He certainly wouldn't have a key to their front door. It was possible the real killers left the door unlocked, which was why the paramedics had been able to get in.

Brian's breathing increased. "I knocked on the door, and when they didn't answer, I looked in through the dining room window. I could see into the living room from there. That's when I spotted a foot sticking out at an odd angle."

If Brian were innocent, Kalan couldn't imagine finding his parents like that. "Did you check to see if the front door was open?"

"No. They were fanatics about locking their doors. Or at least they were when I was growing up."

"Why didn't you call 911 right away?" If he had, and hadn't tried to enter, Brian wouldn't be sitting there now.

"I don't know. I was confused. I ran to the back because I knew where they used to keep their spare key. They hadn't changed its location since I was a kid, so I let myself in and found them." He slipped his hand into his pocket and then his shoulders sagged. "Damn. The key's in my other pants."

"We'll find it then. What did you do next?" He'd have to investigate if the same key was used for the back door as well as the front.

He looked up. "I tried to save my mother. She was still alive so I called for help."

Not the action of a pre-meditated murderer. "I'm sorry, Brian." Until his clothes were processed, along with the bodies, Kalan had no concrete evidence that Brian had killed them. He'd even explained the reason for having the knife in his hand. "You're free to go, but don't leave town."

He bit down on his lip. "I don't want to stay around here. I want to go back home."

"I'm sorry, but I'm afraid you don't have a choice. We shouldn't be that long. Write down your contact information for me and your therapist's number."

Kalan slipped a piece of paper and pencil toward him and Brian jotted down the information.

Sympathy surfaced. If Brian were innocent of the crime, he had to be hurting in his own way. "Do you need someone to escort you back to your hotel?"

"No. I want to walk."

Once he made sure Brian found his way out of the building, dread filled Kalan once more. Having to tell a woman he was fond of that not only had her parents been murdered but that she might have a brother she didn't know about, would rank up there as one of his worst calls ever.

First, he needed to see if his father wanted to do a bit of pro bono work. Brian Stanley seemed like the type to hightail it out of town, and Kalan doubted the department would foot the bill to have him watched. Kalan's dad had not only stepped down as the Beta of the Clan, he'd also hung up his private investigator cuffs, so to speak.

It was close to nine, but perhaps his Dad would be willing to take a late evening drive over to the Silver Lake Hotel.

Chapter Seven

READY TO RELAX after a long day, Elana put away the bottle of red wine and finished cleaning up the kitchen. She'd tried to make some low-calorie snacks but ended up tossing them in the trash. Cardboard would have tasted better and been cheaper too.

Just as she headed back to the living room to pick up a book to read, a knock sounded on her front door, and her heart skipped a beat. No one ever visited after nine. It wouldn't be Izzy as she was busy with Rye.

"Just a minute," Elana called.

Answering the door in a thin T-shirt without a bra wouldn't be cool, so she ran to the bedroom and slipped on a bathrobe. Once she returned, she looked through the peephole and almost screamed. It was *him*!

Elana plastered her back against the door trying to decide how to handle this embarrassing situation. She wore no makeup and the robe she'd grabbed made her look shapeless.

"Elana, it's Kalan. Please open up."

His voice held so much pain it squeezed her heart. Without thinking what she should do, she yanked open the door. Oh, my. He was still in his uniform, looking as hot as ever. When she spotted the clenched hands and a jaw so tight it created lines around his mouth, her stomach did a somersault. "What happened?"

His hair that he usually kept tied back was now loose, yet the man couldn't have looked sexier if he tried.

"May I come in?"

Her manners had evaporated. "Sure. Do you want a drink?" This afternoon she'd purchased a six-pack of beer on the off chance she had the nerve to invite him over.

"This isn't a social call."

As if all of the air had been sucked from her lungs, the delight at seeing him disappeared. "Tell me what's wrong."

"Let's sit down."

Elana was barely able to move. Her mind soared. Nothing would have happened to Izzy, as she was powerful enough to stop a person—or at least in the past she'd been able to. No, it couldn't be Izzy. Rye wouldn't let any harm come to her.

She grabbed hold of the arm of the gold colored sofa and dropped down, motioning him to sit in the flowered armchair. "Tell me. Please."

"I'm not sure where to begin."

Elana sat up straighter. "Just say it."

"I'm afraid your parents were murdered tonight." His chest seemed to sink in a bit, and she swore his eyes turned darker.

Nothing could have prepared her for that statement. "That...that can't be true. You m-must be mistaken. After work, I stopped over at their house. They were... fine." Her vision blurred, and her throat tightened.

"It happened a little after six." Kalan said.

"Are you sure? There has to be a mistake."

Her blood sugar must have suddenly plummeted because the room began to spin, and her body shook. A convulsive sob bubbled up and Kalan jumped up and moved from his chair to the sofa to sit next to her.

He picked up her hands. "I'm so sorry. I know this is terribly hard for you. Losing one's parents can be life altering."

Tears dripped down her cheeks unable to choke out a response. She hadn't realized what their deaths would mean. Sure, they had always been distant, but they had cared for her.

"Do you want me to call someone for you? Izzy perhaps," he asked.

"No. No one. Izzy is busy," she said finally finding her voice.

"I bet she would come if you asked her, or perhaps Mrs. Berta?"

She shook her head as the shakes turned more violent. Kalan leaned close and wrapped his arms around her for comfort, and the tears continued to stain her cheeks. Whether it was for all the things she wanted to tell them or because she'd miss them, she didn't know. Nothing was making sense right now. How could they be dead, and murdered, no less?

Kalan rubbed her back. From the way he was holding her so firmly, it was as if he was grieving right along with her. She leaned back, knowing she looked a mess right now. Her hair was disheveled and her eyes felt as though she'd dumped a pound of sand in them. She swiped a hand across her cheeks. "I'm sorry."

"Don't be." He looked around. "Let me get you some tissues."

Kalan quickly retrieved them from the kitchen counter and returned. She blew her nose and dabbed the tissue under her eyes. "Thanks."

"You sure I can't call Izzy for you?"

"I'm sure."

"Want a glass of water or something?"

She didn't really want anything to drink, but Kalan seemed determined to help make things better. "I'd like that."

Kalan had to open three cabinets before he found a glass. Once he filled it, he returned and handed it to her. The first sip helped quench her thirst. "That's better."

Elana still couldn't believe this had happened. "Who found them?" There was something he wasn't telling her. Her mom's cook had quit a few months ago, so Elana didn't think she'd harmed them.

"A man called it in." He held up a hand. "Here's the strange part. Or at least, it was strange to me when I heard it. He said he's your brother, Brian."

Had she not just swallowed, Kalan would be wearing the water. "I don't have a brother."

The whole world tilted on its axis. She hadn't even accepted that her parents could be dead, and now he was telling her she has a brother?

"He said you'd claim that. Tomorrow, I'll check out his story, but apparently your parents sent your older brother to a mental institution right after you were born."

She shook her head. "Even if I believe they might have done that, why hide the fact from me?" The picture on the far wall of a waterfall began to blur and bile raced up her throat. The deceptions made her want to vomit.

"I wish I had answers for you."

"Where's this man now—the one who claims to be my *brother*?"

"He's at his hotel in town."

This was beyond the realm of the bizarre. She wanted to cry and grieve over this new piece of information, but her stomach was so tied up in knots that nothing was working as it should. At times, she'd believed her parents were monsters, but then they'd do something nice. Like tonight, they'd given her a present, saying the red stone reminded them of her good heart.

She furrowed her brows. "Does he know I exist?" There had to be a reason why she'd never met him.

Kalan looked away, the anguish clear on his face. "Yes."

Why hadn't her parents told her? If he was in town, had he tried to find her? The whole idea that a man claiming to be her brother was at her parents' house and happened to find them murdered didn't add up. "Did he kill them?"

If her parents had sent her away for good, she might be tempted to do them in.

"There's no evidence that he did. When I arrived on the scene, he was trying to save your mom from bleeding out, only he wasn't able to."

Another sob erupted and Kalan rubbed her shoulder, helping to soothe the intense ache. "Did he say why he was there?" she choked out.

"He wanted to talk with them again."

Numbness encased her, and her stomach threatened to revolt. Kalan once again wrapped his arms around her and held her tight. As much as she enjoyed his strength and warmth, she needed answers more than sympathy. Elana leaned back. "Why did someone kill them? They didn't socialize. Hell, they weren't even in town very often." More tears streamed down her cheeks, though the grief had yet to sink in.

Kalan's hold tightened. "I'll figure it out. I promise."

It almost wouldn't matter if the criminals were caught. Her parents would still be dead. They'd never see her one flower shop turn into two and then three. Nothing she could do now would make them proud. Elana sucked in a sob, but she wasn't sure if it was because she wouldn't see them again, or if she no longer had time to prove to them she was worthy of their love.

Kalan sat back. "It's my job to ask you where you were around seven thirty tonight?"

Elana swiped a tear from her cheek and almost laughed. "You think I could have killed them?"

He grit his teeth. "No, never. You have a kind heart, but all relatives are suspect."

She sniffled and tried to remember when she'd spoken with Izzy. "Check my phone records. I think Izzy and I were chatting about that time." Hopefully, he wouldn't ask about what.

He brushed away a lock of her tangled hair from her face and tucked it behind her ear. "I'm sorry, but I had to ask."

"I know." If he believed she might have done such a heinous act, he wouldn't have held her.

"Listen, I would stay with you, but I have to get back to work."

She didn't want to burden him with thinking he needed to watch over her. "Oh, of course." Being alone wasn't what she needed though. "I'll call the Bertas."

"I'd feel better if you do."

Her true grief had yet to sink in. "So would I."

"How about you pack a few things and I'll take you over there? I don't want you to have to tell them what happened by yourself."

He was so nice. "I'd appreciate that."

As Elana stood, her legs gave way, but Kalan reached up in time to help ease her descent onto the sofa seat.

"Take it easy and rest a bit. There's plenty of time to pack. I'll stay with you for as long as you need me."

She almost swooned at his wonderful attitude, but a wave of grief prevented it. "Thank you, again." Elana sipped on her water, her mind spinning. "Why would someone kill them? Or did I ask you that already?"

"We suspect it was robbery."

"Robbery? What were they after?"

"We're not sure. We might have you look around to see what's missing."

Her gut cramped. She wasn't sure she was even capable of stepping foot in the house again. It never held good memories, and with them gone, it might be worse. "They changed a lot of things after I moved out."

"Perhaps a visit right away won't be necessary."

Being around Kalan was messing with her head. Breaking down in front of him had been ugly. "I need to pack."

This time when she rose, she was able to make it to her bedroom. While she kept a suitcase in her closet, figuring out what to take overwhelmed her. She didn't even know if Izzy's parents were home, or how long she'd stay if they were. If she called them, she'd have to explain why she needed to come over for a few days.

Elana collapsed onto the bed and sobs wracked her body. She'd never felt so alone in her life.

"Need help?"

Elana jerked then sat up as she wiped at her cheeks. "I'm having a bit of difficulty figuring out what to pack."

"Why not take two of everything, and then you can return in a day or two to pick up more?"

"Good idea. I guess if I need anything else, when I come to work tomorrow, I can pick up a few more things."

Kalan sat next to her on the bed. "I'd rather you not go to work tomorrow."

Her heart beat too fast. "Why?"

Clasping her shoulders, he leaned in close—too close—and her mind blanked for a bit.

"I want you safe. I'm not saying for sure that these people will come after you, but they were looking for something, and it's possible they didn't find it."

"Whatever it is, I don't have it, and even if they told me what they wanted, I wouldn't know where to look. It's been years since I lived there." She moved out of his grasp, his presence unnerving her. "I'll see if Anna can work all day tomorrow."

"Good. Remember, two of everything. I'll be in the living room when you're ready to leave."

For some reason, Kalan's instructions helped, and within minutes, she was all packed. With case in hand, she stepped out of her bedroom.

Kalan jumped up from the sofa, rushed over, and lifted the suitcase from her fingers. "I'm sure if you forgot anything, Mrs. Berta or Missy can walk across the street and pick it up for you."

"Are you always this nice?"

He smiled and a ray of sunshine lifted her spirits. "Only for a beautiful woman."

Izzy was right. He was a playboy, but what a nice playboy he was.

Kalan helped her into his cruiser and then headed toward Wendaya Cove. He must have known where the Bertas lived because he pulled into their driveway without asking directions. Fortunately, the lights were on inside, implying they were home. Izzy's wonderful parents were more like a mother and father to Elana than her own folks had ever been.

"Thank you for being the one to tell me what happened. Having a friend deliver the news helped ease the pain somewhat." Having that friend also be her dream man was a bit unnerving, yet comforting at the same time.

"I wouldn't have let anyone else do it."

With Kalan by her side, Elana was convinced she'd make it through this.

He helped her out and when they rang the bell, Kathryn Berta answered right away.

"Elana? Kalan? Did something happen? Is Izzy okay?" Her gaze shot to the suitcase in Kalan's hand.

"Izzy's fine," Elana said.

"Then come in, please."

The large, two-story Berta house was like what a home should be—warm and welcoming. While their furniture had more of a country flair than her parents' place, and the Berta home was full of knickknacks and photos of the family, instead of purchases from an overseas' art gallery, it exuded safety—both for her person as well as for her heart.

For the next hour, Kalan explained as much as he could about her parents' murders. Throughout it all, Len and Kathryn remained stoic, though Elana hadn't expected them to grieve over her parents' deaths. If it weren't for Izzy, Missy, Len, and Kathryn, Elana might have ended up in an institution too.

As soon as Kalan left, Kathryn Berta called Izzy, Missy, and Teagan to let them know what had happened.

Mrs. Berta returned from her calls. "Missy is with something and can't come over, and Izzy isn't picking up."

"That's okay." Elana wasn't sure if she wanted to retell the story many more times.

Kalan had been gone no more than ten minutes when Teagan rushed in. Her blonde hair looked like she hadn't combed it before rushing over, and her print shirt didn't match her brown jeans.

"Oh, Elana, it's my fault." She slid down next to her on the sofa and picked up her hand. From the haunted look, and slightly yellowish tinge to her skin, Teagan had had another vision.

"I don't know what you're talking about, but nothing was your fault."

She glanced to the side. "A few weeks ago, I had a vision that something would happen, but I didn't say anything because it was so brief. It occurred right after that man tried to kidnap Izzy."

The pressure in Elana's temple nearly exploded. "What did you see?"

"As I said, it was brief—so brief in fact that I had to sit down and try to re-envision what I saw." She looked across the room as if trying to bring back the image again. "You were surrounded by darkness. That was all at first. I tried to force my mind to bring up more of the vision, but it didn't work." She returned her focus back on Elana. "I realized it would occur sometime in the future, but it could happen weeks or maybe months from then."

"Why didn't you say something?"

"Say that something bad could possibly occur? With no time frame, it would only cause you to be anxious. No, I didn't want you to worry."

It was true that if Teagan had said something bad would happen in the future, Elana would have been looking over her shoulder, doubting everything she did. Elana had no doubt that Teagan was looking out for her best interests. "I get it. I really do."

Teagan clasped her hand. "I'm still worried about you. There's no guarantee that the evil is gone. That's partly why I'm here. I had another vision this evening, only this time it was bad—like the one I had when Izzy was being held captive."

Sludge pooled in her veins. "Are you saying the killers might come after me now?"

"I can only tell you what I saw. You'll have to judge for yourself."

Part of Elana didn't want to ask, but her life depended on her knowing. "What was it?"

"I'll explain the best I can, but it made no sense to me. I saw what looked like you standing in a field in an unknown location. Instead of you being human, though, you were made of a hard, highly polished stone. Then what looked like a twister came roaring at you, but before it could hit you, something big and fast blocked the path. Then you returned to your human form."

Now what was she supposed to make of that?

Chapter Eight

KALAN WASN'T HAPPY about leaving Elana for a few days, but someone had to find out about Brian Stanley and whether he was capable of murder. The mental institution where Brian was treated was in Ohio, a six-hour drive from Silver Lake. While it was a long haul, it gave him time to think about a lot of things, especially Elana's vulnerability. It weighed heavily on his mind, and the urge to protect her distracted him. If only his damned body would stop reacting when he was around her, he could come up with a plan on how to find the killer and keep her safe.

Women had always been a delightful diversion—nothing more—but ever since he'd run into Elana, his world had been turned upside down. At first, he thought it was the stress from taking over for his dad, but now he wasn't so sure.

Mate, mine.

Kalan's bear was making him anxious and it was pissing him off. The damn animal kept pushing and clawing at him whenever he was close to Elana or even thought about her. Kalan just wasn't ready for a mate, which was why he kept forcing his bear to back down, shoving the whole mate thing out of his head the best he could.

As nice and wonderful as Elana was, he'd been led to believe he was destined to be with a bear shifter. Perhaps, he should just show his true self to her and watch her run away screaming. That would end their alluring relationship fast.

Before he could even consider stopping what had never really started, he needed to solve her parents' murders, and that meant he had to find out everything he could about this dysfunctional family.

With only an hour's drive left to the mental hospital in Ohio, he called his dad on his hands-free Blue Tooth set to check on Brian's whereabouts.

"Brian's been staking out Blooms of Hope, but don't worry, I've got my eye on him."

Good thing there weren't many cars on the road, or he might have crashed into one. His nails extended and his protective nature shot to high alert. "Elana isn't at the store is she?"

"I'll make sure nothing happens to her."

"Dad, I asked you a question." His father could be annoyingly tight-lipped at times.

"Elana came in about an hour ago and hasn't left."

"Damn woman. I told her to stay with Izzy's parents."

"Both of whom are across the street from her store. I'm thinking it might be safer for her to be here than alone at the house."

He had a point. "Let me know if Brian tries anything—or leaves town."

"Got it under control, son."

If he didn't trust his father completely, he'd have been tempted to turn around and ask his questions of Brian's therapist by phone. Kalan had discussed the pros and cons of driving up to visit the facility where Brian had been treated versus calling the doctor with his boss, but they both felt a face-to-face discussion would provide him with the best information. There might even be others he could speak with.

His appointment with Brian's therapist wasn't for another two hours, but he'd intentionally left some time to drive around for a bit so he could get a better sense about the institution.

In need of some caffeine first, he pulled into a coffee shop parking lot. Easing out, he stretched, ready to get this interview over.

Once he purchased his coffee and a small snack, he sat at an outside table and called Elana, needing to make sure she was okay.

The air in the Ohio Valley was muggy, causing sweat to pool on the back of his neck, but he didn't need people overhearing his conversation.

If he warned her that Brian was skulking around, it might prompt her to approach him, and that was the last thing either of them needed.

"Kalan, are you okay?" she asked answering on the first ring.

Elana's worried reaction made him smile. "I was calling to check up on you. I can take care of myself."

"So can I."

No one was within earshot so he could speak freely. "Really? I was unaware that you had magical talents." Like her best friend.

"Didn't I mention that I'm a martial arts expert and have a shelf full of sharp shooting trophies?"

She was cute. He couldn't have been more pleased that she was able to joke at a time like this. Perhaps, it was her way of coping. "No, I didn't. I guess I don't have to worry about you then."

"You don't have to go that far. I like hearing from you."

While he was pleased with her comment, it made him uncomfortable at the same time, because she was slowly worming her way into his heart, and he wasn't prepared for the consequences. "So, is it strange being back at the Bertas' house?"

Kalan was curious how far she'd go to keep her current location a secret.

"I'm sorry, Kalan. I couldn't stand being there by myself. I was going stir crazy. I had to come into work. I'm comforted being around my flowers."

The sudden rush of anxiety had him clutching the coffee cup so hard some spilled over. "I wish you hadn't."

"Anna is here with me, and Len has come over about ten times, as have Kathryn, Missy, and Teagan."

"I'm glad to hear it. I'm about to interview Brian's therapist to see if I can get some answers. I'll be back in town tomorrow, and I'll stop in to see you."

"Really?"

She acted as if he didn't care about her and that bothered him. He might not be interested in something permanent, but he did enjoy being with her. *Stop lying.* He wanted her—and so did the bear inside him. "Yes, really, now stay out of trouble."

"I will. I'll see you tomorrow."

"Okay. You be careful driving home after work."

He disconnected the call. Just speaking with Elana made his pushy bear return. Keeping that animal in check was getting harder. And that wasn't the only thing that was getting harder. *Fucking hell, I am so screwed.*

BRIAN'S THERAPIST LOOKED older than Methuselah, but from all the credentials on the wall, he was highly qualified.

"I'm very sorry to hear about Brian's parents. This is going to set him back," Dr. Patterson said.

"I don't understand why? You said he was suffering from attachment disorder. I'm no therapist, but if he can't really relate to them, why would he be upset if they were dead? Brian said he hadn't seen them since he was eight. And secondly, why did he try to save his mother if he wasn't close to her?" That was probably too many questions to throw at the man at once, but Kalan's anxiety levels had risen ever since his call to Elana.

"Detective, Brian is not a monster. He has issues, as do many children who are raised in and around an institution, but he possesses some compassion. I was the one who suggested he speak with them to bring some closure. I was hoping they could provide some insight as to why they thought it had been best to send him away when he was young."

"Was it best?"

He blew out a breath. "For a while, yes, but if his parents had been willing to care and love him, he could have moved back home. I don't believe he would have harmed his sister, or anyone for that matter. When I spoke with them, I found them to be cold and arrogant."

Kalan's heart ached for Elana. Without the support of Izzy and her parents, no telling what kind of woman Elana would have become. "In your professional opinion, do you think Brian could have killed them?"

"No. Not unless something triggered it. Just so you are aware, Brian is bipolar, but when he is properly medicated, he functions just fine in society. He works at the local lumberyard here and seems to be doing well. He doesn't interact with customers and that suits everyone involved."

Well, shit. Kalan was no closer to an answer than before. He asked a few more questions, but the doctor didn't provide any further insight. Kalan saw no reason to wait around to speak with the others since Dr. Patterson had provided a list of names he could contact as references for Brian. "Thank you for your time."

"I'm sorry you drove all the way up here."

He wasn't. The long drive gave him some time to think and put things into perspective. "I might be calling you again."

"Anytime."

Bottom line, Brian Stanley was a sad anxious man who had been dealt a bad lot in life. While it was possible something happened in Silver Lake to make Brian snap, it wasn't looking like he was guilty, though Kalan wouldn't rule it out. Stranger things had happened.

While he had planned to spend the night in Ohio and drive back to Tennessee tomorrow, after speaking with the doctor, Kalan didn't want to be away from Elana longer than necessary.

Before he took off, though, he called Dalton and filled him in on what he'd learned. "I'd appreciate it if you'd keep an eye on Elana. Just so you know, I've asked my dad to help too. Her shop won't close for another hour, so if you could make sure she gets back to the Berta's safely, I'd appreciate it. But keep a low profile. I don't want her to think that something's wrong."

"I've got your back."

"I owe you."

As he headed south to Tennessee, Kalan sifted through the facts of the case. If he assumed Brian was innocent, who would be the next most likely suspect? Elana's parents were in the import-export business, so perhaps they'd cheated a client or failed to deliver on a promise. With them dead, he wasn't sure how he'd find the information, and he doubted Elana knew much about their dealings.

As he crossed the Ohio border, his cell rang. A quick glance indicated it was Finn McKinnon, Rye's brother. He couldn't remember the last time he'd even spoken to him. If he wasn't in the middle of a murder case, Kalan might have let it go to voicemail. He tapped his ear piece. "Hey, Finn, what's up?"

"Sorry to bother you, but I heard about the murders."

As much as he liked Finn, he wasn't about to give out any details. "How did you hear about them?" Most likely, Elana told Izzy who told Rye, but there would have been no reason for Rye to mention it to his brother.

"Bartenders hear everything. When I found out it was the Stanleys who'd been murdered, I remembered having a conversation with a guy who was asking about them."

Kalan gripped the wheel and concentrated on the road. "What did he look like?"

"He was about five feet ten, short, dark brown hair and a little chunky."

"That was probably Brian Stanley. He's their son."

"I know. He came back the night of the murders and told me."

Finn was tossing too much information at him at once. "Back up and start from the beginning."

"The first time the guy came into the bar, he asked where the Stanleys lived. He said he was a business acquaintance and was passing through town. I liked the guy. He was super polite and tipped well, despite only having one drink."

"Did he say anything else?" An exit appeared ahead, and Kalan took it. He pulled into the gas station at the corner and parked, wanting to jot down what Finn told him.

"He wasn't at the bar for long the first night, but when the guy came in the second time, he was loud and a bit inebriated already. I had to water down his whiskey."

"Was he talkin' trash or something?"

"You could say that. Brian told me he was the Stanleys' son and that he'd come back to Silver Lake to tell them what he thought of them once and for all."

Acid burned in his stomach. He couldn't believe someone would tell all that to a bartender. "What time was this?"

"I started work at six and he came in maybe forty-five minutes later."

"How long did he stay there?" Brian had called 911 around seven-thirty.

"Not long. Maybe half an hour."

That meant he had enough time to get back to the house and kill them. "I appreciate the intel, Finn."

"You bet."

Kalan disconnected, more confused than ever. Needing another caffeine hit, he rushed into the convenience store at the gas station and bought a coffee that he hoped wasn't stale. Once back in his car, he placed the drink in the cup holder to let it cool first.

He was still having a hard time reconciling the look on Brian's face when he was with holding his mother to that of a cold-blooded murderer. The therapist implied Brian might have harmed his parents only if something triggered the rage.

Well, shit. Once he drank some of the coffee, which turned out to be quite palatable, he returned to the highway. With one arm over the wheel, he leaned back and almost had to squint at the bright light from the moon. While it wasn't a blood moon, it had been one a few days ago.

Oh, fuck. Kalan hadn't even considered the Changelings might have been involved, even though he'd detected a shifter signature in the house. While he'd never witnessed one of them taking the form of another human, the timing sure was right. The only problem with his theory was when would they have run into Brian? Lore had it that a Changeling had a seventy-two hour window around the blood moon to touch a human and then transform into that person.

With so many unanswered questions, it was good that he was returning home tonight. He pressed his foot on the accelerator. If the cops stopped him for speeding, he'd flash his badge and say it was a matter of life and death—Elana's.

Chapter Nine

ELANA WAS IN her pajamas sitting on the bed with Missy who'd insisted on staying at her parents' house to keep Elana company. In high school, it had been her and Izzy, because Missy was two years younger and was usually banned from their older girls' convo.

A cloud of guilt hung over Elana for not grieving more, but right now, Elana wanted to forget the horror and concentrate on something pleasant—like catching Kalan Murdoch's eye. "I can't believe I broke down in front of Kalan. And trust me, I'm an ugly crier."

"He'll understand."

"I hope so. Now, I'm just numb. I don't think I could cry if I wanted to."

Missy reached out and clasped her hand. "People grieve in different ways. I know this isn't the same thing, but when I was in maybe seventh grade, one of my classmate's dogs had passed away. I knew she loved that animal more than anything, but the next day she acted as if nothing had happened. Then about three months later, she was reading a story and started bawling her eyes out. Something in the passage triggered the memory of her dog's death and that was how she reacted."

Missy was always trying to soothe the way between people. "I appreciate that. Everything is still surreal—especially finding out I have a brother. Your support and your family's have been wonderful. I don't know what I would have done without you all."

Missy scooted across the bed and hugged her. "You have Kalan too. He seems to want to protect you."

"I hardly *have* Kalan even when he's around, but I'll admit it's nice to be able to focus on something new and fresh, even if it is only temporary." She wasn't so naïve to believe that men like him stayed with one woman for long.

"I think that's smart. So are you going to work tomorrow again?"

"Yes. Kalan said he will be back in town, and I bet he stops over. Keeping busy helps me stay sane."

Missy slid off the bed and straightened her T-shirt. "I'll let you get some sleep then. If you wake up and need someone to talk to, I'm here."

"Thank you." With Kalan in her dreams, she'd make it through the night.

EVEN AFTER WAKING up several times from her erotic dreams, Elana actually felt moderately refreshed in the morning—or else it was the extra strong coffee Kathryn had made for her that had done the trick. As soon as Elana got to work, she planned to call Teagan and ask if she'd had any more premonitions, even though she wasn't totally buying into the whole statue vision thing. Elana was unaware of any kind of magic that could turn a human into a rock, though it was possible the stone was some kind of metaphor.

"You can stay at the house if you want," Izzy's mom said. "Or you can go into work. I know that solitude can often be daunting."

"I appreciate that. I want to keep busy."

"We'll make sure to keep an eye out for you then."

Izzy's parents were too good to her. Why couldn't she have been born into this family instead of hers? Most likely, the adversity had made her work harder and created the desire to start her own business.

When it was time to leave, all four of them piled into Mr. Berta's car. Now that Kalan would be back in town, Elana felt comfortable returning to her own apartment, but she'd broach that topic with him after work.

Len Berta dropped her off in front of her building. "I'll stop by later and make sure you're doing okay."

Len was very protective of his family, and to deny him the ability to help wouldn't allow him to show how much he cared. "I appreciate it."

Elana entered through the front door then locked it behind her. Before she opened for business, she needed to go up to her apartment. Last night, her hairbrush had snapped in half while brushing her unruly hair, and she needed to find her spare.

For some reason, the air seemed to have a stronger flower aroma than usual, and the scent calmed her ragged nerves.

After taking the back staircase, Elana was about to unlock her door when she noticed it was already ajar. What the hell? Pinpricks of fear stabbed her, and her stomach twisted into knots. Had she left it unlocked when Kalan had escorted her to the Bertas? She hadn't even ventured upstairs yesterday because she hadn't needed anything.

"Hello?" Her voice cracked, and her jaw wobbled. If someone was in her apartment, it was probably dumb to call out, but her brains were too scrambled to think straight.

When no one responded, Elana pushed the door open and gasped at the destruction. Cushions were torn, pictures that had been straight were now askew, and her kitchen cabinets were all open. Her heart jackknifed and then her blood pressure plummeted, forcing her to grab onto the doorjamb for support.

As much as she wanted to go inside and check it out, it was as if she had turned into some kind of marble statue. Unable to move or think, she stared for at least thirty seconds before the adrenaline kicked in, and she was able to function once more.

Warning lights flashed in her brain. *Run!*

As fast as she could, Elana raced back down the staircase fearing her intruder was still inside. When no one seemed to be following her, she slowed, but then thought if no one was upstairs, whoever had done this might return. She had to leave.

She unlocked the front door to the store, checked that no one was near, and dashed across the street. She then burst into Len's vacant cellular phone store.

"Elana, what is it? You look like you've seen a ghost?"

Her heart was hammering in her chest so hard it was difficult to get the words out. "Someone broke into my apartment."

"What?" Len rushed to the front store window and glanced across the street, though she had no idea what he thought he might see. He spun around. "Are you okay?"

Emotionally, she was devastated. Two shocks within two days were too much to take. It was wearing her down. "Yes."

"I'm contacting the sheriff's office."

"Okay. I'll call Kalan. He should be on the road heading back to Silver Lake."

For some reason, she thought he might know what to do. He had hinted that whoever had killed her parents might come after her for something, assuming he hadn't found what he was looking for in the first place. *Shit.* Her purse was across the street, along with her phone and Kalan's number that he'd written down after he'd taken her to the Bertas.

Len nodded to her. "I'd like to report a break-in." He explained what she'd told him. "Elana Stanley. Sure. Yes. I didn't realize he was back in town. Thank you." Len disconnected. "Seems your fella drove back last night. They said they'd contact him."

The blood rushed from her head. "Kalan's here?"

"Seems so."

He must have returned late last night, and relief coursed through her just knowing he was close by.

Len led her over to the stool behind the counter. "I want you to stay right here. I'll make sure nothing happens to you," he said.

While she'd never seen Len shoot fire from his palm like Izzy could, her friend had claimed her father's aim was quite remarkable. That was good enough for her.

Less than fifteen minutes later, a rather bedraggled Kalan rushed in. The top few buttons of his beige uniform were undone, and it looked as if he hadn't shaved this morning—unless his scruff grew really fast. From the haunted look in his eyes, one would have thought it had been his place that had been broken into. "Elana, are you okay?"

Before she could respond, he had her in his arms. She almost cried at the comfort of being in his embrace. "No one harmed me physically, if that's what you're asking, but emotionally, I'm having a really hard time with it."

"I know, it has to be difficult. You must feel violated."

"Yes." She hadn't been able to pinpoint the exact emotion, but that description fit perfectly.

Kalan stepped back, sliding his hands down her arms to her hands. "Tell me everything you remember."

She described how Len had dropped her off at the store and that she immediately went upstairs only to find the door ajar. "I didn't even think. I just pushed open the door, but I didn't go in. I was so scared that I ran back down and came here. I wanted to call you, but I left your number in my purse that's back at the store." She covered her mouth. "I left the front door to my store unlocked."

"You stay here and let me check it out. I'll have our forensic team in right away. Do you have any idea what they might have been after?"

"No." But hadn't he previously said it might be the same thing the murderer wanted from her parents?

Kalan turned to Izzy's dad. "Len, can you stay with her while I check out her place?"

"Absolutely."

As much as Elana wanted to go with Kalan, she didn't want to get in the way. "Can you bring my purse back?"

"Sure. What color is it?"

"Pink. I left it on the counter." She only planned to be upstairs for a minute. As much as she needed her brush, she wouldn't ask him to look for her extra one.

"I hope it goes with my outfit." He smiled, but she could tell it was for her benefit.

"Go."

This nightmare didn't seem to have an end in sight.

As Kalan stepped into Elana's apartment, he halted. Holy crap. The gold colored sofa was torn up, drawers were tossed on the floor, and some of the artwork on the walls was either knocked to the side or onto the floor. This level of destruction was reminiscent of her parents' home. While he had no proof, it appeared as if the same thief had destroyed both. Thankfully, Elana wasn't home at the time or she might have been killed too.

Working hard not to let his bear out, he stepped into her apartment, careful not to touch anything. He detected a wolf scent along with cigarette smoke that he was sure hadn't been there the other night.

He immediately called Phil Smythe and mentioned his theory about the intruder being the same person who murdered her parents.

"Does she have any idea what they were after?"

"No."

"I'll send forensics over. She might be their next target. See if she can stay someplace safe."

He had just the location, though heaven help him if he'd be able to control himself. He could ask the Berta's to take care of her, but if a Changeling were involved, even the Bertas' magic wouldn't be enough. "Yes, sir."

He'd have to ask his the Clan council to help decide how to proceed.

Before the CSU team showed up, he contacted his dad. Silver Lake had been relatively calm until Brian Stanley had come to town, and Kalan wanted to check if Brian was anywhere near his sister's apartment this morning or last night.

"Dad, I'm calling to check on Brian's whereabouts."

"All's quiet on this front. He hasn't left the hotel this morning."

He wondered how his dad knew that. "Are you sitting outside his room or something?"

"Not exactly."

He waited for an explanation, but one wasn't forthcoming. Sometimes his father drove him crazy with his round about answers. "Someone broke into Elana's apartment and tore it up bad, rather like the way it was done at her parents' home. Thankfully, she wasn't here. I wanted to make sure it wasn't Brian."

"It wasn't."

"How can you be so sure? The B&E could have occurred in the middle of the night."

"It wasn't Brian. Look, it's better if you aren't aware of my tactics. Just remember what I did for a living."

Oh, fuck. His dad probably illegally planted a camera in the man's room. "Dad?"

"You said this was important."

He had said that, but his father needed to remember his son was a cop. "Let me know when he leaves."

"Will do."

No sooner had he hung up than the forensic team arrived. Not wanting to be in their way and needing to get back to Elana, he told them to contact him if they found anything important.

Feeling a little self-conscious carrying a pink purse, Kalan tucked it under his arm and raced across the street to where Elana had her face pressed against the window. She should know better than to expose herself like that. Just because her parents were stabbed didn't mean this killer didn't own a gun. He entered the store and handed her the bag.

"Thank you."

He thought about tossing out a snarky comment about how good he looked in pink, but then decided now wasn't the time for levity. "Why don't you move back behind the counter?"

She turned around, trudged to the middle of the store, and sat down on the stool. "Did you see anything?"

He'd seen a lot. "You mean did I see anyone?"

She dragged her hair away from her face. "No. I mean, could you tell anything from all that mess what he might have been after? I didn't go inside but I looked. I was hoping maybe he'd left a note or something."

"I think that only happens in movies. I didn't touch anything, but the crime scene unit is there now. If there are any fingerprints that don't belong, they'll find them."

"I think I can guess what you're going to say next. I won't be able to go back to my apartment or go into work."

Poor Elana. It was as if he was cutting out her heart. "I'm going to make it even tougher on you. I think you should close your shop all together for a few days. I'll send someone in to clean up the mess so you won't have to deal with it. The department hires a service for this purpose, and the Bertas can keep an eye on the storefront. I'll ask the department to install an alarm system tied directly to the office too. That way we'll know if anyone tries to break in again." McKinnon and Associates Security would give the department a good deal on the equipment. If Phil balked at the expense, Kalan would pay for it. He understood how much the store meant to her.

"That's really nice of you, but that means Anna doesn't get paid."

Neither would Elana. "I'm sorry."

She looked over her shoulder. "Len and Kathryn said I can stay at their place for as long as I'd like."

The problem with that was they might not be able to stop a Changeling from snatching Elana or killing her, especially during the day when they were at work. How he was going to convince her that he was capable of taking care of her without giving away he was a bear shifter was anyone's guess, but he had to try. "I think you'd be safer at my place."

Her chin tucked in, acting as if he had two heads. He could see her point though. The Bertas had magic on their side to help protect her, while she believed he was a mere human.

"Why? You'll be at work all day, and I'll be just as vulnerable to attack there as I am at the Bertas."

He had to tell her something. "I live near Rye. I don't have to work tomorrow and Rye might be able to take off the next few days. You'll be closer to Izzy—at least in the evening." He hoped that would sway her.

She bit down on one of her nails, and Kalan found himself actually holding his breath. His human side wanted her to say yes because she'd be safer in the shifter's compound, but the animal in him just plain wanted her. It might be wiser to have her stay with Mr. Berta at his store during the day because Kalan's inner bear was already acting up. Then again, if the Changelings were involved, she'd be an easy target here too.

"I guess I could stay with you, but do you have room?"

Now wasn't the time to come back with a smart aleck remark about how his bed could easily accommodate both of them. "I have a spare bedroom."

She glanced back at her store. "Okay, but I'll need to pick up my suitcase from the Berta's."

"I can drive you."

"I'm guessing with the CSU team still there, I can't go back to my apartment."

With every roadblock he was tossing her way, he could feel her slipping away. "Not right now."

"Do you want to go now?"

"Yes." But goddess help him, if this might not be harder on him than it was on her.

Chapter Ten

ELANA WAS CONFLICTED. She was about to go to her dream man's house and stay under the same roof with him. She should be elated at the offer, but Elana couldn't be sure of his motives. It would be too good to be true if he wanted to keep her safe because he really cared for her. As a lawman, it was his job to protect.

Kalan first drove her to the station, where he dropped off his cruiser then picked up his Jeep, implying he would stay the day with her, and not return to work.

"Have you ever had to put someone in protective custody like this before?" she asked.

"You mean has anyone stayed at my house because they needed protection?" She nodded. "Never."

Okay, that put things in a different light. Then again, maybe no one had been in imminent danger before. It wouldn't be smart to focus on his motives, as she couldn't afford any more disappointments.

Once in front of his house, Kalan put his Jeep in park, turned off the engine, and unsnapped his seatbelt. The outside of his cute one-story home was brick with white trim, complete with a small front porch. The grass was freshly cut and the shrubs in front were all neatly trimmed. He seemed to own quite a bit of land, though there were several nice homes in the neighborhood close by, including Rye's.

"You really do near to Izzy and Rye."

"Not only does Rye live down the street, his family and my whole family live nearby too. It might be why we've been best friends since grade school."

How wonderful to have grown up surrounded by a ton of kids, especially brothers and sisters.

Kalan escorted her inside, and she immediately felt at home. The living room, dining area, and kitchen took up the front of the house, which was compact and cozy. A hallway off the living room led to what she suspected were the bedrooms.

She'd grown up in a place where her parents made her take off her shoes in the wintertime for fear of tracking in snow and dirt. Even when they weren't home, those in charge of her made sure she did as they had demanded. While her mom was a fan of flowered material and stripes on her furniture, Kalan's design was simple—dark browns and black. It had a definite masculine flair to it.

If she lived here, she would have added something other than sports memorabilia on the wall, but he was a bachelor so it made sense. "This is really nice."

"I'm not into decorating, but it serves my purpose. Let me show you the spare bedroom. You'll have to use the hall bath if that's okay. I have my own in the master so we won't have to share."

Sharing wouldn't have been all that bad. She might even get to glimpse him naked, or at the very least, see him with a towel wrapped around his deliciously damp body. Kalan placed a hand on her arm, jolting her out of her reverie. "Oh, thanks."

He escorted her down the hallway and into a decent-sized room that didn't look anything like the rest of the house. The comforter on the queen-sized bed was a thick duvet done in pinks and greens, and four large pillows leaned against the headboard. The watercolor over the bed was of a lush waterfall surrounded by deep forest greens, very different from the photos in the living room. "This is amazing."

"You can thank Blair. She feared that if our cousins from up North ever visited and there wasn't room at my parents, they'd freak if they had to stay at my house given the way I'd furnished it."

"You have a nice family."

"I do indeed."

A knock sounded on the front door and Kalan stiffened. "I'll be right back. Stay here."

Elana had held up quite well over the whole breaking and entering thing, but the way Kalan commanded her to remain in the room tightened a band around her chest. She closed the door and locked it in case someone had followed them. Just because Kalan had said no one had, didn't mean this intruder hadn't avoided detection.

A moment later, someone tapped on her door. "Elana, it's me, Izzy."

Relief weakened her knees and she unlocked the door and tore it open. In seconds, she was hugging her best friend.

"Dad just called me and told me what happened, so I hurried right over." Izzy wrapped an arm around her waist. "Come sit in the living room and tell me all about it. I can't believe you have to deal with yet another tragedy."

Once they were seated, Kalan brought out some iced tea. "Mom made this last night and thought I could use some."

Elana looked up at him. He seemed to be trying hard to be a good host. "Thank you."

"While I change out of my uniform, you two chat."

Once he was out of sight, Izzy faced her. "You'll be safer here than at my parents' house."

That wasn't what she expected her to say. "Why's that? Because they need to be at work during the day?"

She glanced to the side as if she was hiding something. "Rye isn't the only werewolf around."

Elana had figured that much out, though she'd never asked who was a *Were* and who wasn't. Then it hit her. "Is Kalan one?"

"No, but Rye's family are all werewolves, and they live close by. They can help protect you. His father is retired and said he'd be willing to come over here when Kalan has to go to work."

"That's so sweet of him. I'm happy to stay here until the forensic team finishes with my apartment, but then I'd like my life back. I do have a store to run. My flowers can only live so long without care."

Kalan wanted her to stay away for days, but she couldn't afford the loss in revenue.

A small smile lifted Izzy's lips. "My powers are not gone, you know. I can keep the flowers alive if you want."

"I appreciate that, but that isn't the point. I enjoy working." She sagged against the seat. "I'll go stir crazy sitting around here all day worrying if he'll come after me—whoever *he* is."

Izzy cocked a brow. "Perhaps you can convince Kalan to stay home and *entertain* you."

"Izzy! It isn't like that. I'm staying here so he can protect me."

"Protection can take a lot of different forms." Her friend winked.

"You're a hopeless romantic."

Izzy looked down the hallway to where Kalan had gone. "I know the circumstances suck, but aren't you a little impressed that Kalan wanted to bring you to his home to protect you?"

"It's his job."

"I'm not so sure. I asked Rye, and he said Kalan has never brought anyone home before who has needed protection."

"He told me that too. Kalan is going out of his way to be nice, but he seems to have some hidden agenda, only I can't figure out what it is."

"He probably doesn't know how to act around you."

"What do you mean?"

Izzy clasped Elana's hands. "He's probably afraid of saying the wrong thing and upsetting you more. You've just lost your parents and now you've been robbed."

Robbed? "Do you know something I don't? I never went inside to see if he'd taken anything."

Izzy released her grip. "No, but usually when someone breaks into a place, it's because he wants something."

"I wanted to go back and look, but Kalan wouldn't let me."

"Do you think you're ready to handle seeing another violation?"

Her friend was probably right. "I guess not." She leaned her head back and sighed. "You know what really sucks?"

"More than what you've already been through?"

"Yes. The last time I saw my parents, they were acting really nice to me." Izzy's eyes widened. "I know, right? They even gave me a present. Let me show you. It's in my room. I'm not exactly sure what to make of it."

Elana rushed back to the bedroom and snatched her purse off the bed. As she stepped from the room, she glanced at the closed door down the hall, wondering what was taking Kalan so long. Most likely, he was giving her time to be with Izzy. That was nice of him, though she wasn't sure she wanted him to turn into Mr. Polite. In her dreams, he'd been anything but.

When she returned to the living room, she opened her bag, lifted the six-inch long piece of highly polished red onyx, and held it out. "Mom said they picked it up in India for me because it reminded her of my good heart."

"That's really nice." Izzy fingered it. "Did she say what this was used for over there?"

"I think it's just a decorative piece. My folks collected stuff like that all the time. They have a green marble pyramid about four-inches tall that they purchased in Egypt, and a gold-rimmed stone they found in South Africa. They have no purpose except to look pretty."

Heavy footsteps sounded down the hall. When she looked up, her breath caught at Kalan's rugged good looks. His sandy colored hair was wet and he was clean-shaven, but perhaps it was the white T-shirt outlining his muscular body that instantly switched her from sad to glad.

"What do you have there?" Kalan strode over to her.

"It was a gift from my parents."

He held out his hand. "May I see it?"

Izzy gave it to him. "It's sardonyx," Elana said.

"Nice and heavy." Like Izzy, he ran his fingers across the surface, but his gaze seemed far away. "When did you get it from them?"

"Just a few hours before they were murdered."

His brows pinched. "Did they always bring something back with them for you?"

"No, but maybe with them getting older they wanted a better relationship with me. I was hoping anyway." She looked off to the side and threaded her fingers together. Just thinking that her parents might have wanted to mend things between them brought on fresh tears.

Kalan said nothing about her outburst as he flipped the sardonyx over then back again, for which she was thankful. Izzy handed her a tissue from her purse, and Elana dabbed her eyes. "Thanks."

"There's something about this that seems familiar. Do you mind if I keep it for a few days? I promise to give it back."

As long as he returned it, she was good. "Sure."

"Izzy, is Rye home?" Kalan asked.

"Yes."

"Do you think Elana could stay with you for an hour or so? I have an errand to run."

"No problem." Izzy stood and looked down at her. "Come on."

If Kalan hadn't sounded so intense, she would have asked if she could come along with him. Guess she'd just have to trust him.

Because the day was so pleasant, Izzy had walked over, and they headed back the same way. Even though the houses weren't too far apart, Elana couldn't help but glance around, expecting someone to jump out at her.

"I think we should have an aura cleansing in your apartment," Izzy said.

"What good will that do?"

"Didn't you listen to anything Mom said while we were growing up?"

"Of course, but I don't see how that will help if it was an attempted robbery." Kalan said he was going to find someone to clean it up so she didn't have to see everything they'd destroyed.

"I wish this hadn't happened, but once Mom does her magic, it won't feel creepy being in there." Izzy opened the side door to Rye's house and let them in.

Elana sighed. "Okay."

Izzy smiled and gave her a nod, silently letting her know she would do anything to help her feel safe.

"You don't lock your door?" Elana asked.

Izzy shook her head. "Rye's here. Nothing can harm us."

Perhaps werewolves had more powers than she realized. Rye came out of a back room and rushed over to her, gently gripping her shoulders as he looked into her face. "Kalan told me what happened. I'm so sorry." Rye wrapped his arms around her, giving her a supportive hug. "How are you doing?"

"As well as can be expected, I guess."

"How about some cookies to munch on?" Izzy asked.

Elana slipped from Rye's grasp and followed Izzy into the kitchen. Her friend grabbed one of the two tins on the counter and opened it.

Izzy looked over to where Rye was seated. "Rye, did you eat all of the cookies?"

"Guilty, but there's another tin. Eat those."

Pink colored her face. "Well, crap."

This wasn't like Izzy. "What's wrong?"

"Have a seat." Elana plopped down on the stool in front of the island. "Remember when I took you to Ophelia to do a spell to rid Kalan from your head?"

"A lot of good that did." Elana could think of nothing else now. If anything, her obsession had grown worse.

Izzy leaned her elbows on the counter. "About that. I really believed that you and Kalan would make a cute couple, and I wanted to give you two a chance to get to know one another."

Elana lowered her chin. "Isadora Berta, what did you do?"

"I asked Ophelia to put a slightly different spell on you than what you asked for."

"Izzy, spill it."

"You are such an amazing person and I wanted to give you the gift of self-confidence around Kalan."

Elana was speechless. Of late, she had been more comfortable around him and had been rather brazen in her thoughts. "A spell? How long is this spell supposed to last?"

"Maybe forty-eight hours, though it could be a week. I really don't know."

From her lack of eye contact, something else was going on. If they hadn't grown up as close as sisters, she might not have recognized the signs. "What else did she do?"

Izzy blew out a breath. "You know how Kalan always seemed so out of sorts around you? Running into doors? Dropping things?"

Her wording almost made her laugh. "You mean how he always tried to run away from me?"

"I believe he was trying to come to grips with his intense desire for you."

Elana threw up her hands. "Now you're being ridiculous. I might believe he likes me, and maybe even cares for me, but desires me? No way."

"Regardless of what you think, Ophelia gave me some herbs to put into some chocolate chip cookies I made for Kalan. It was supposed to make him less clumsy and nervous. It allowed him to be himself around you."

"That was really sweet of you to try, but he still acts odd a lot of the time whenever I'm near. Is that what's in these cookies?" She nodded to the second tin.

"Yes. I wouldn't chance eating them if I were you." Izzy tossed them in the trash.

Just as well. She didn't need anything else to mess with her head.

Izzy leaned her elbows on the counter. "All I ask is that you keep an open mind."

Now her friend was talking nonsense. "About what? The fact that he might like me?"

"About everything."

Now what the hell did that mean?

Chapter Eleven

HAPPY TO GET out of the house, Kalan headed directly toward James's cabin on the other side of Silver Lake. Being with Elana was causing his bear to revolt. He wanted her bad. Even when he was in the bedroom changing out of his uniform, he yearned to mate with her.

Shit. This was so hard. Elana didn't have any idea his kind existed. Wolves, maybe, bears no. What would she think of him when she found out he'd omitted the fact that he was a shifter? But damn, he was protecting her from the harsh reality of life. Somehow, he sensed she wouldn't see it that way.

Forcing his bear to retreat, he focused on what was in his pocket. From the moment he touched that stone, Kalan had an uneasy feeling that it was somehow connected to what was happening in Elana's life.

James had been able to provide guidance and good intel when Izzy had been captured by that horrid Changeling, and Kalan hoped the immortal could provide some answers about this stone too.

With an unsettled feeling lodged deep in his gut and the sardonyx in hand, Kalan knocked on James's door. He probably should have asked his Alpha to join him, but he needed him to watch Elana. While the rose quartz at the bottom of the lake would dilute the Changelings' powers if they came around, he didn't trust them not to attempt to overpower the girls should they not sense Rye close by.

The door opened, and James motioned him in, acting as if he

knew what Kalan was going to ask him. His Alpha claimed the man was creepy like that. No one knew for sure the extent of his powers, but since he was married to a goddess, he might possess a lot.

"What can I do for you?" James ushered him into the stark living area where an unlit fireplace dominated the stone home. Facing the hearth were several pieces of furniture that looked handcrafted from some very large trees, probably carved during the last century. Worn cushions were on the seats of the sofa and chairs.

Kalan was too agitated to sit. "Did you hear about the Stanley murders?"

"A real shame. How is Elana holding up?"

He knew her? "As well as can be expected. Do you know why her parents were murdered?" Rye seemed to think James was omniscient, and Kalan wanted to test that theory.

"No."

Whether he was telling the truth or not was anyone's guess. Kalan retrieved Elana's parents' gift from his pants pocket. "Do you know anything about this stone?" He'd heard that the Changelings valued it highly, though he didn't know why.

"Where did you get this?" James lifted the gift from Kalan's fingers and examined it.

"The Stanleys brought it home for their daughter. They gave her the present hours before their death."

As if James were hundreds of years old, he edged over to one of the chairs and dropped down. He motioned Kalan to do the same. Not wanting to inhibit the flow of conversation, Kalan obeyed.

"I've been hearing rumors that the Changelings powers are slowly diminishing."

Kalan sat up straighter, his pulse erratic. "What exactly does that mean?"

"I'm not sure. Their ability to shift won't be affected, but several of the members have powers similar to the Wendayans—at least for a short while."

His gut twisted in half. "I've heard they can take the form of another human if they come in contact with them around the red moon, but that's all." Dear goddess, if they could control fire, wind, water, and other elements, no telling what havoc they could wreak.

"I've heard otherwise," James said. Kalan waited for him to explain but instead of continuing, he stood and returned the stone. "Do you think this was what the murderer was after?" James asked.

"I have no idea."

"There's a Changeling by the name of Chris Darden who might know. My sources overheard mention of Chris purchasing some special sardonyx from the Stanleys. This type of stone is rare. See the light streaks through it? It's the density of the colors that affects its availability."

"What exactly would the Changelings want with the stone?"

"To restore their powers, of course."

Of course? Who else knew about this? "Which powers?"

James shrugged and pressed his lips together as if nothing could pry them apart. Perhaps Chris would be more forthcoming with information.

"Here's Chris's home address," James said, pulling a piece of paper from his pocket and then standing.

Something fishy was going on, but Kalan wasn't in a position to demand answers. "Thank you."

James escorted him back to the front. As Kalan pulled open the heavy wooden door, James lifted a finger. "Elana is still in danger, so protect her at all cost."

His pulse soared. "From whom?"

"I suspect the killers."

James knew more than he was sharing. "Then what can you tell me about Brian Stanley, Elana's long lost brother?"

"Nothing." James waved a hand, acting as if her brother wasn't a threat, but Kalan wasn't convinced.

He'd had enough of this evasive bullshit. "Why are you hiding things from me?"

"Me? Why would you say that?"

"Because you had already written down this Chris person's address before I even arrived. Why can't you tell me what you know?"

James blew out a breath. "Fine. Come sit down again and let me explain something to you."

He wanted to return to Elana, but at the same time, he needed to find out what James knew. Kalan stopped in the middle of the living room and crossed his arms over his chest. "Tell me."

"You are so impatient and demanding. That's not a good trait for a Beta."

Tough shit. The woman he was falling in love with was in danger, and James was not cooperating. "I'll deal."

Did he just say love? His bear must have put those thoughts in his head.

"Please don't think I don't want to help you. I do, but I am held accountable to those higher up." He glanced at the ceiling.

Kalan stilled. "You were told not to help mortals?"

"I didn't say that. I'm allowed to give you a little nudge now and again until you get on your feet, so to speak. Like when that Scottish Changeling kidnapped Izzy, I pulled some strings to find out what happened."

"You saved her life."

"I'm glad. You want your mate to be free of danger too, so I've provided you with a name that should lead you to the killer. You'll have to do the rest."

Now Kalan felt like he was eight again when his parents had punished him for shifting into his bear form and running through the house, breaking some furniture. "I appreciate all your help."

"Talk to your dad and Rye's father. They went through the same learning curve. I provided some much needed help at first until they learned to help themselves."

Kalan stuck out his hand and shook James's hand. "I will."

Halfway back to his house, he suddenly recalled James's words. He'd said Elana was his mate. So it was true. Or was it another lie? No. Whenever he was near her, he wanted her worse than anything.

His denial at first had caused him to run away, but his need to protect her now was so fierce it had to be true. Even if he were willing to mate with her, he still needed Elana's consent and he doubted that would come easily.

Kalan's cell rang, jarring him. It was his partner, Dalton. "What's up?"

"You won't believe what happened."

"What?" Elana was safe and that was all that really mattered.

"Someone broke into Brian Stanley's hotel room and trashed the place."

Oh, shit. "I'll be right there." He disconnected and immediately called his dad. "Where's Brian?"

"Whoa. Slow down, son. Brian's at McKinnon's Pub."

He had to assume it was the real Brian if his dad was tailing him. It would be curious to see what Finn thought of this man as opposed to the one who had come to the bar drunk the night of the murder. "Dalton called and said Brian's motel room was trashed."

"Well, damn. I usually go home for lunch to check the camera feed because Brian pretty much stays in his room. When he left and came to McKinnon's Pub I decided to have lunch here to keep an eye on him."

"So you have a camera in his room."

"Guilty."

As much as he wanted to rant at his dad, he was now grateful his father had set up surveillance in the room. It might provide the possible identity of the killers. "I'm heading over to the hotel now. While I'm checking it out, how about looking at those tapes and let me know right away?"

"You want me to leave Brian?"

If Brian's room was trashed, it helped exonerate him from the murders. "Yes."

"I'm on my way. I'll get back to you." His dad disconnected.

Kalan immediately called Rye. He would have used telepathy, but Rye might have had some difficulty explaining to Elana he knew something when his phone hadn't even rung. "Elana's brother's room was vandalized. I'm heading over there now. Please tell Elana I'll be back when I can."

"I'll keep her safe."

"You better."

"THAT WAS KALAN," Rye said, stepping over to the kitchen island. "Apparently, someone broke into Brian's hotel room and trashed the place."

Acid burned her stomach. "Is he okay?"

Rye lifted one shoulder. "Kalan didn't say, but he would have mentioned it if Brian had been there."

Her quickened heart rate slowed. She might never have met her brother—at least that she remembered—but she didn't want something bad to happen to him before she did. "That's good. Does that mean Kalan wants me to stay here?" If so, perhaps Rye could walk her back to retrieve her gear.

"I don't think he plans to be long. He just asked that I make sure you stay safe."

Part of her was thrilled Kalan was taking such good care of her, but another part was shaking. If he needed Rye to watch over her, Kalan must suspect the killer planned to come after her.

Izzy closed the lid on the now empty cookie tin. "I think we need to make some more. You want to help, Elana?"

"I'd love to." Anything to keep her mind off what was happening.

As if Izzy had lived in Rye's home for months, she located all the pots and pans and set out the ingredients with efficiency. "I really do love the powers that I have, but if I could wave a hand and create a scrumptious meal, life would be so much easier."

Elana laughed. As kids, they used to talk about their fantasies—and boys, of course. "I want to wave my hands and have my shop squeaky clean."

Izzy pointed a finger at her. "Now you're talking."

For the next hour, they mixed the batter, baked the cookies, and then waited for them to cool before sampling each batch. Elana's hands were in the soapy water cleaning up when Kalan walked in. His gaze latched onto her as if he was impaling her with a beam of sexual energy.

She quickly glanced over at Izzy, wondering if her friend had slipped in some of that secret ingredient Ophelia had given her into the cookies.

"How did it go?" she asked, working hard to keep her voice from cracking.

Kalan dropped down onto the center island stool. "I could use a cookie or two if you can spare some. I'm starving."

She didn't like that he'd avoided answering her question. "You are such a man."

He grinned, but it appeared as if that took some effort. "I try."

Izzy handed her a plate, and she filled it up with at least a dozen chocolate chip cookies and placed it in front of him. "Here you go."

Rye came over and sat next to him. "Tell us what you can."

"This is not for public knowledge," Kalan said, "but I asked my dad to keep an eye on Brian since I wanted to make sure he didn't come after Elana."

Elana planted a hand on her chest. "I hope he isn't involved in any of this."

"It doesn't look like he is. Before my father retired, he worked for a security firm run by Rye's dad. My father seemed rather unsettled after he returned from his retirement cruise, so I asked if he could help. No surprise, he jumped at the chance. What I didn't expect was for him to put a security camera in Brian's room. He wouldn't tell me how he managed it, but he probably slipped the maid some money to let him in the room."

Her breath caught. "Does that mean you have the trespassers on camera?"

"Yes and no. I just spoke with my dad and he said both men

wore masks."

That didn't make sense. "If they walked down the hallway in masks, surely someone would have seen them."

He shrugged. "My partner is there now knocking on doors."

Kalan eased off the stool. "You ready to head back to my place? I'm in need of some real food."

"Sure."

Izzy picked up the plate of cookies. "I'll put these in a bin for you to take home."

Kalan held up a hand. "Oh, no you don't. Last time I ate the whole batch in like two days." He patted his stomach.

"Suit yourself."

Elana hugged her temporary bodyguards goodbye. Being surrounded by her friends, even if it was for a short while, helped keep her from falling apart. When Elana stepped outside, to her delight, the fear that had blanketed her since her parents murders had mostly disappeared. Being around Kalan gave her such a sense of well-being.

Even though dusk was falling, the summer air was still muggy. The crickets and cicadas were going crazy, along with several bullfrogs. Those around Silver Lake truly lived in the country.

"If Brian is supposedly in the clear, do you have any other suspects?" she asked.

An adorable smile crossed his lips. "First off, I can't discuss the case with you any more than I have. And secondly, how about we forget everything for one night and try to relax?"

She wasn't sure she was capable of ignoring the pain in her chest, but she'd try. "You want to watch TV or something?" There was so much she didn't know about him and so much that she wanted to learn.

"How about we talk while we eat?"

"What do you want to talk about?"

Sex or their possible relationship? Even she couldn't help but notice the sly looks of yearning that were often followed by a glare as stoic as a rock. It was almost as if he was trying to gain control, but why?

"Anything you want. I have some hot dogs in the fridge. I could build a fire, and we could cook them outside. How does that sound?"

Her heart lurched. Most families went on camping trips or at least set up a tent in the backyard and roasted marshmallows over an open fire. Hers did not. "I'd love that. The last time I did anything like that was when I was in ninth grade, and Izzy and I went to the annual bonfire that signified the start of football season."

"I loved those times. After the game—win or lose—the team would go to someone's house and drink all night."

"In high school?" That slipped out. Just because she wasn't a party hound, didn't mean he hadn't been.

"We were stupid back then." He slowed as he neared his house. "You never went to parties?"

Tension rippled through her. Now he'd think she was some social outcast. "My parents were often out of town and didn't want me going out."

"You went with Izzy the first time. Why not again?"

She looked up at him and smiled. "I guess it won't hurt if you know. That first year, Izzy kind of had a crush on one of the linebackers and wanted to make an impression on him. It was right after you graduated, I think. The guys on the team decided to see who could build the biggest blaze. When it was Justin's turn, Izzy kind of helped."

Kalan laughed. "Did anyone find out she was the one who lit the fire?"

"Some might have suspected, especially when she raised her arms and caused the wind to fan the flames."

"Any repercussions?"

"No, but her desire to help Justin win the contest backfired—pun intended. Every girl at the event surrounded him when he was declared the winner. After that, we didn't go. I think Izzy was afraid her magic would slip out."

When they reached his front door, he held it open for her. The moment she stepped inside, she was wrapped in a sense of being home. Funny how certain rooms could draw you in like that.

"You want to change?" he asked. "Even with a fire, it can get a bit buggy by the lake. I suggest a long sleeve shirt and some pants."

She liked that Kalan seemed so concerned for her. "Good idea."

"Wait." He retrieved her red onyx from his pocket. "I'd feel better if I put this in the safe. Are you okay with that?"

He was being silly. "My parents would never buy me anything that valuable. I'm sure there's a ton like it in India."

"Maybe, but I want to be cautious."

As her father used to say, one man's trash was another's treasure. "Okay."

When Kalan disappeared, she headed to her room to change. When she returned, he was organizing the hot dogs, paper plates, napkins, and matches on the counter. He then stuffed them in a garbage bag. "Ready?" he asked.

Good thing her mom couldn't see this adventure. She'd be horrified. "Where are we having this feast?"

"I thought we'd go by the lake because there are several fire rings already made. With so many trees around, we need to be careful."

This whole spontaneous outing put her in a much better mood. A few clouds graced the sky, but there didn't seem to be any rain in sight. The path was secluded, safe, and peaceful. "It's so nice here. Even though we live in Silver Lake, I've never been."

"That's not surprising as the land, including the lake, is privately owned. This whole area was purchased long ago by some developer, and most of the families have lived here a long time."

"I had heard that, but since I love being around the water, I wish I had been invited."

"Do you like to swim?"

The idea of wearing a bathing suit gave her the willies. "No. Izzy was the swimmer. I'm not into sports."

"You seem to like walking."

Without thinking, she punched him in the arm. "That's not a

sport."

"It is if you do it fast enough."

She supposed that was true. They turned down a path, and when the lake appeared she was filled with awe. Rays from the last of the sun made the water appear almost iridescent. "It's fantastic."

"It's one of my favorite places. There's a kind of solidness to the lake."

That was an odd comment. "Water is hardly solid."

"The bottom is supposedly lined with pink quartz which is what gives the lake its shimmering surface. I feel the lake is solid, metaphorically speaking, in that it won't drain away and be gone someday."

The last thing she expected from Kalan was introspection, but she liked it.

He stopped. "This place okay?"

A fire ring was set back about fifteen feet from the water's edge, and someone had dragged several logs and placed them around the circle for seating. "Perfect. What would you like me to do?"

"Gather some sticks, but make sure they're already on the ground."

"We should have invited Izzy. She could have lit a fire with nothing but her magic."

He smiled. "I like to do it the old fashioned way. It's a guy thing."

Kalan turned around and Elana couldn't help but stare at his ass. He was wearing jeans and looked damn good in them too. A wave of desire washed over her. *What the hell? Get a grip Elana.* She was in mourning and Kalan was here to protect her, not be eye candy. She needed to focus on the task at hand before she did something stupid like reach out and grab his butt.

For the next ten minutes, she gathered small sticks along with some slightly larger ones. When she returned, Kalan had a stack of large pieces off to the side. "Where did you find those?" she asked.

"Found them at another fire ring." He slipped the wood from

her fingers. "You know how to build a campfire?"

She laughed, and it actually sounded full of cheer. "No, my family wasn't the outdoors type."

With great care, he explained how to place the medium sized twigs in an alternating square fashion. "Once we've built a six-inch high log cabin structure, we'll place some dried leaves inside and then place the tinder on top."

While he constructed this special wood fort, she broke off the small pieces and dropped them inside. When all was set, Kalan was able to light the fire with one match, and Elana clapped. "You're good."

"You ain't seen nothin' yet. Wait until you taste these dawgs." He picked up one stick, withdrew a knife from his pocket, and whittled the end into a sharp point. "Perfect."

Kalan insisted she sit while he prepared the meal. With both hotdogs jammed on one end, he rotated them over the crackling fire until the skin nearly burst. The scent of burning woods, the rich pine from the forest, along with the aroma of the lake almost made her high from the collective smells.

"All done." With short, quick movements, he pulled off the first one, dropped it on a plate, and handed it to her. He then removed his.

She wasn't sure how she was supposed to eat it without a bun though. Using her fingers was totally out of her comfort zone, not to mention, the meat was hot. Kalan had placed his hotdog on his paper plate with one end sticking off the edge, folded the plate in half like a bun, and bit into the end.

"Something wrong?" he asked with his mouth full of food.

"No. Everything is good."

Take a chance. Go for it. For the first time since she'd learned of her parents' deaths, a sense of freedom engulfed her. The first bite was better than anything she'd ever tasted. Elana didn't know if the wood made the difference or if it was because of the carefree man next to her that made things more appealing.

"You ever take any trips?" he asked after he polished off the first hot dog and stuck a second one on the stick.

"Trips?"

He smiled and her insides did a little somersault. "When was the last time you took a vacation?"

"Not in a long time. My parents were out of town on business so much that they didn't have time to take me anywhere." God, now she sounded like a real loser. She should have lied. "After I finished college, I didn't have the funds to go anywhere."

"Then imagine your time at my place as a trip to another land. You said you haven't seen this lake, so pretend you're in a different place."

Kalan had a great way of looking at things, so different from her logical mind. "I'll try that."

While he ate two more hot dogs, she studied the surrounding beauty, loving how the fire sent soothing heat to her front. An occasional blue jay would squawk and the cicadas would suddenly go silent then flare up again. As the sun set, the nearly full moon appeared, and the beams skipped across the small waves in the lake, creating a dreamlike atmosphere.

"Ready?" Kalan asked.

Elana jumped. She'd been lost in thought—good ones for a change. "Yes."

He dumped some dirt on the fire and stomped out the embers. Kalan placed the garbage and uneaten food back in the trash bag, making the carrying process easy.

About halfway back, she was looking up at him when her foot hit something sticking up from the ground, and she tripped.

"Whoa!" As if he possessed lightning fast reflexes, he steadied her. "Gotta watch where you're going."

Was he kidding? "It's dark out here. How can you see?"

"I have Superman vision." Before she could respond to his mocking comment, he clasped her hand. "You're safe with me."

Holding hands seemed natural to Kalan, but to Elana, it was a new experience. He wasn't acting like a cop, but rather like a man who liked her. Several times during their cookout, she'd caught him staring. If she hadn't been so stressed out, she'd have believed his facial hair had actually grown thicker and his nails had become longer. She'd blink, he'd look away, and then everything would return to normal.

Kalan led her into his house and then dumped the trash. "You want to watch a movie?"

As much as she would have enjoyed snuggling up against him, she was really tired. "Would you mind if I just showered and dropped into bed?"

"No problem. If it will make you feel safer, you can lock your door, but I'll be here to protect you."

His sincerity touched something deep inside her. Without thinking, she wrapped her arms around him. "Thank you."

Before she did something she'd regret, Elana rushed down the hall. Her goal right now was to get through the night.

Chapter Twelve

KALAN WAS PLEASED Elana wanted to head straight to bed. If she'd been willing to watch a movie with him, he might not have been able to keep from ravishing her. His bear was growing stronger by the hour, pushing, clawing and chanting *mate*. He was constantly trying to hide his body's reaction whenever he was near her. Hell, his claws kept coming out, his hair had sprouted a few times and teeth had sharpened. Even worse, his damn cock never seemed to go down, and he could only run to the bathroom so many times to get himself under control before she started to wonder what the hell he kept doing in there. Christ, she probably already thought he was some kind of weirdo.

James had stated Elana was his mate, and Kalan was finally ready to admit that it was true. He could no longer deny it, and his body sure had been sending out confirmation signals ever since he'd run into her.

He'd thought about going back to James and asking him if he knew why he'd been paired with a human, but the closed-mouth man would probably shrug and say he had no idea. It wasn't as if James couldn't ask his wife, since Kalan assumed an immortal and a goddess could communicate telepathically. If they couldn't, the thirty days they were forced to spend apart each month would be terribly painful.

The bathroom shower turned on and Kalan's senses shot to high alert, forcing his bones to crack. As he pictured Elana naked in his bathroom rubbing soap over her large breasts and between her legs, it was almost too much to bear—no pun intended. No amount of self-control seemed to be working, and he was all too aware that she was too fragile for the type of sex he needed. Hell, even if she hadn't been recently traumatized, it would scare the shit out of someone as sheltered as she had been.

Kalan paced, trying to figure out how to handle this insanely intense desire that he had for Elana. A mate! He never would have guessed, but he was damn glad she was the one.

His protective side was pummeling him from the inside, and his urge to mate appeared to be doing some internal damage as well. Doing so her right now, however, was out of the question. He'd only approach her if she acted first. Since that would never happen, he'd have to suffer in silence and hope his bear didn't succeed in taking over.

The door to the bathroom opened. He turned to look out the window instead of glancing back down the hallway, forcing himself to think about work. One look at Elana wrapped in a towel, and he would have lost it.

When the door to her bedroom closed, he let out a breath then waited until the lock clicked. Once he was convinced she was snug and safe in her room, he grabbed a beer from the fridge and dropped onto the sofa.

From his pocket, he took out the address of the Changeling who might know something about the murders. The handwriting looked like something one would find on an ancient sea scroll, written in ink with long flourishes at the end of the letters. Kalan didn't recognize the address because the Changelings rarely called the sheriff's department for help. Driving around the mountains was asking for trouble, so he'd avoided it when possible.

Tomorrow, he'd ask his dad to keep an eye on Elana while he and Rye checked out this Chris Darden fellow. Even if this guy wasn't responsible for killing the Stanleys, he might provide some useful information—or not. Changelings weren't known for their generosity.

Kalan stretched out on the sofa ready to keep vigil over Elana. If anyone tried to sneak in, they'd have to come through him first. The Changelings' powers weren't strong near the lake, but they could cause trouble. If a human had been responsible for the deaths, Kalan bet that person would die of a heart attack if Kalan shifted into a seven-foot bear. No, Elana would be safe on his watch.

Needing to relax, he turned on the tube. By midnight, however, the drivel on the television made him nearly comatose. If he slept in his room tonight, and someone managed to break in, they might reach Elana before he did.

There was only one solution. Shift into his bear form and sleep in front of her door. He'd rise as soon as the sun came up, and she'd never be the wiser. His biggest fear was that once he was in his bear form, though, he'd want to break down the door just to be with her. His human self had some control, but he wasn't sure about his animal side.

He left the television on with the sound off, hoping to make an intruder believe he was still up.

Kalan shifted and then spread out in front of her door. As much as he believed he would fall asleep quickly given how fatigued he was, he found it hard to calm his racing thoughts. Elana's little whimpers tempted him like no other. He prayed she didn't cry out, for if she did, he wasn't sure what he'd do. For now his bear seemed to be satisfied with at least being allowed out to protect her.

If he didn't get some shuteye, however, he wouldn't be able to protect even an ant tomorrow. Eventually, his mind shut down and his body succumbed to a deep sleep.

The full body impact and scream woke him. *What the hell!* He opened his eyes to find Elana on top of him, scrambling to get off. *Oh, shit.* He didn't dare move for fear of further startling her. Only then did it occur to him that she might have wanted to use the bathroom in the middle of the night—the one that was across the hall from her room. Stupid…stupid. His hormones had blocked his thinking process.

Once she managed to climb off him, Elana rushed back into her room, mixing whimpers with screams of *Oh my God* and *Stay away*.

Fuck. She slammed the door, and he shifted back into human form then knocked. "Elana, are you okay?" That was a stupid question, but he wanted her to speak to his human half. Then he'd tell her he was the bear in front of her door.

Suddenly, the door flung open and Elana grabbed his arm to pull him into her room. She then slammed and locked it once more. The next thing he knew, she threw herself in his arms then leaned her head back looking up into his face with scared wild eyes.

Seconds later, she released him and frantically paced the room not paying any attention to him. She waved her arms around. "There's a bear out there. Didn't you see him? We need to get out of here." Elana was headed for melt down, and he needed to do something.

"It's okay, calm down. We're safe. I promise."

She edged her way toward the window and clicked on the light next to her bed. When she swung around, her eyes became as large as the white moon.

"What's wrong? I won't let anything happen to you, trust me."

"You're…you're…naked."

Oh, fuck! He'd completely forgotten that when he shifted back to human form he wouldn't be wearing clothes. Of course his cock had no problem showing just how happy it was to see her. Kalan clasped his hands in front of his cock and balls, but it didn't help much, not with Elana dressed in an adorably thin T-shirt that had her perky nipples poking through just begging him to suck them. Add in her loose pajama bottoms, and he was hotter than the fire they'd lit tonight. "How about I put on something?"

He opened the door and she rushed toward him. "What about the bear?"

"The bear's gone," he said walking back to his room. He was botching this badly, but he wasn't going to have a conversation when she was gawking at him, and he was pretty sure right now she was staring at his ass.

"How is that possible?"

He just needed to tell her. Taking a deep breath, he turned around to face her. "I was that bear."

She stared at him like he had two heads. Kalan rushed back to her, ready to calm her down.

All of a sudden, a broad smile split her face. "You're a werebear?"

Her gaze dropped to his hands that were once more trying to cover his junk.

"Yes," he said hesitantly, shocked at her wide eyes and the joy in her voice. His bear was pushing hard from the inside, forcing his incisors to sharpen and hair to sprout on his body.

"Ohmigod. I know Rye is a werewolf, but I had no idea bear shifters even existed."

"Well, we do, but I'm a bit confused by your reaction. You aren't scared? Or even surprised?" His voice deepened.

"No. I'm excited. This is so cool. Can you shift back for me?"

The joy in her voice caught him off guard. As his brain tried to catch up and comprehend what she had asked, he stumbled with his words. "What…Why?"

"I love bears. They're one of my favorite animals, so big and cuddly. Izzy said Rye is really sweet even when he's in his wolf form."

Sweet? He doubted the Alpha would appreciate that label. "We're not vicious in our animal form if that's what you're asking." He stepped back. "I'll go change."

"Yes, change into a bear."

Was she crazy? Her mind must have scrambled from the shock. Elana hadn't even been aware his kind existed, yet she seemed to accept it. Having grown up with the Wendayans probably helped. "Are you sure?"

"Yes."

From the gleam in her eye, returning to his bear form would delight her even more. He couldn't help but shake his head. She was practically giddy about finding out he was a werebear. Never had anyone had that kind of reaction to him before.

This can't be good, but since Elana was his mate, he'd do it. Steeping back, he did what she wanted—he shifted.

THE SIGHT BEFORE Elana overwhelmed her. Kalan Murdoch really was a bear. How cool was that? She couldn't decide what part of him she should touch first. She'd had a love affair with animals from a young age, but her parents had steadfastly refused to let her have a pet, saying they were too messy and too much trouble. No amount of arguing had swayed them. After she finished her schooling and moved out of the house, she'd decided against having one, as she'd been too busy getting her business off the ground.

Now she was actually standing in front of a real live animal—and what a glorious creature he was. Standing, he was a good seven feet and quite imposing. His fur was a dark brown and shiny, except around his mouth, where it was streaked black and white. He had a long and sleek snout, but his black nose was compact and cute. Kalan made a handsome bear.

With caution, she stepped out of her room and faced him, keeping her back to the living room. "Kalan can you understand me?"

Izzy said Rye could understand her when he was in his wolf form, but she also said that once they mated, they were able to communicate using only their minds, but that seemed like science fiction to her.

He gave a huffing sound and nodded his head. Yes!

Believing the human Kalan was inside the large bear, she walked behind him to test his reaction. Bear Kalan didn't move. "Can you get on all fours for me?" she asked as politely as she could.

What sounded like a low growl came out, but he did as she asked. Even in this position, he was huge, but that wasn't going to stop her from fulfilling her fantasy. Grabbing hold of his coarse fur, she bent her knees and sprung up onto his back, his body more muscular than she'd expected. As soon as she was seated, he moved forward as if he wanted to take her outside.

"Not too fast," she said. She petted his head, loving the silkiness of his fur. "Nice."

This time his growl turned even deeper. Instead of heading for the front door, he lifted up and she gently slid off, thankfully landing on her feet. "Whoa."

Fur flew and what sounded like bones cracked. A blurry whirlwind later, Kalan was back in his human form—and gloriously naked too.

The smile she expected from him wasn't there. "I hope you had some fun, but I need to explain something to you," he said in a stern voice as he stalked towards her, towering over her. "I am not a pet. You may touch me all you want, but I am still a man who has wants and needs. You're little riding exercise has caused my hormones to explode, and if you don't want some hard loving right now, I suggest you run and lock your door."

Holy crap. Elana couldn't move. For years, she'd dreamed of this moment, but this serious side of Kalan scared her in its intensity. It also made her juices flow. "Okay."

He stopped and clenched his fists. "Okay, what?"

I'd like to make mad, passionate love with you. "I'd like to kiss you."

Kalan closed his eyes and groaned. "I couldn't stop at one kiss if I tried. The moment you say yes, beware I might lose control."

Those words resonated deep within her. Until now, she hadn't realized how much she truly wanted and needed this man—to breathe, to think, to be happy.

"Yes," she said, her heart pounding so hard she feared it might burst from her chest.

Clasping her shoulders, he walked her backward until she ran into the wall next to the front door. As much as she wanted to look deep into his gorgeous eyes—eyes that seemed to be changing from hazel to amber—she wanted to gaze at his cock even more.

Kalan grabbed her hand, his palm rough and calloused, and placed it on his super long, thick shaft. Elana had slept with a few men, but none were anything like this. "You're so big," she said as she hesitantly ran her hand up and down its length.

"The more to satisfy you with." This time he graced her with quirked up lips that turned his rugged good looks into a highly sensual one.

He cupped her face and kissed her with what was probably restraint for him, but what was to her an amazingly take charge kind of kiss. She released his cock and dragged her hands up his back, mapping out every ridge and muscle. Elana couldn't touch him enough. Kalan must have sensed her desperation and wrapped his arms around her, drawing her close, and then running his tongue along the seam of her lips. Passion and desire swamped her and she opened up. The moment their tongues came in contact, she could actually taste the minty toothpaste from when he had brushed his teeth earlier. As their breaths increased, so did the pressure on her chest. She dragged her hands back down his rippled back, loving the play of his muscles each time he moved or ran his hands up and down her butt.

Kalan broke the kiss. "Need you naked now."

Oh, God. Did he really just say that? Given he was so large in his bear form, she hoped he'd appreciate her larger-than-life size. "Umm, ohhkay."

Elana hated that she hesitated in her response, but suddenly she was nervous and unsure how to proceed. He was already naked—thankfully. If she'd had to take off his clothes, she might have melted into a big puddle of goo on the floor. Just the sight of his glorious was body was making it hard to think clearly.

"I need to warn you first," he said.

That made her a little nervous. "About what?"

He huffed out a breath. "The longer we stand here, the harder it will be for me to stay in my human form. You know nothing about what we shifters go through once our bodies tell us that we have to have you. If you see my eyes change color or my facial hair grow, it means I'm about to shift, and I really don't want to do that, but damn, it's hard not to."

Elana was speechless. The whole concept that a man would want her that much blew her away. "Can I touch you?" She reached out to him.

"I don't think that would be a good idea, at least not this first time."

This first time? Did that mean he wanted her for longer than tonight?

"What would you like me to do?"

"Keep your hands at your sides."

A giggle escaped. *Gah.* She was a twenty-seven year old woman, not some virginal teenager, so she shouldn't be shocked at the idea of sexual attraction. He slipped his fingers under her T-shirt, and when he dragged his palms up to her breasts, she actually shuddered with pure lust and desire.

"So nice and firm and round. I bet they taste sweet too," he said.

"You won't know unless you try them." Where that boldness had come from, she didn't know. It must have been a residual effect from that witch's spell.

Elana wasn't sure what possessed her right then, but she reached out and ran her hands up his hard abs. A strong visceral reaction to touching such hardness left her panting. As if Ophelia herself was in the room guiding her, Elana's hands then lowered until she ran into the tip of his cock. It felt like warm velvet but hard as steel at the same time.

Grab it.

Just as she was about to, Kalan clasped a hand around her wrist and put her arm back to her side. He raised his eyebrow giving her a look that told her to leave it there. He then slipped her shirt up and over her head.

"Exquisite," he said.

She was about to say sucking on his cock would be exquisite too, but all words flew out of her head the second his tongue touched her nipple with his finger. Bending over, he squeezed one breast, rolling the nipple between his thumb and forefinger. At the same time, he performed a circle dance with his tongue around the other while giving little nips to the tight bud. If she hadn't been leaning against the wall, she'd have had a hard time staying upright as her knees were starting to give out.

"You sure I can't touch you?" she asked as her hands fisted, digging her nails into her palms.

"Fine, but don't freak out by what you might feel." Then he winked at her.

She giggled, catching his double entendre. "I'll go slowly."

Elana didn't want to be distracted from the glorious bliss coursing through her, but on the other hand, seeing him struggle to keep control would be such a high—one she'd never experienced before.

His glorious locks were begging her to run her hands through them. So she did. The silky texture was a stark contrast to the coarseness of his animal fur, and his hair was lighter in color.

He looked up at her. "I don't know how long I can last." His eyes were glowing amber now and his scruff had turned fuller. "You are just so beautiful."

Don't dispute it. "So are you." She pulled her hand along his shaft again, running her thumb across the tiny slit gathering some moisture then glided it around the edges of his cock head.

"Holy Fuck! You've had your fun. Let's go."

In one easy motion, Kalan lifted her up and strode down the hallway. Elana couldn't help but laugh. No man had ever carried her.

His bedroom was dark, but the door was open. As soon as he stepped in, he set her down then flicked on the light. Kalan walked over to the table next to his bed and pulled open the drawer. "Need one of these."

His king-sized bed was unmade, but the rest of the room was neat. One long dresser graced the wall opposite the bed, and a chair sat in the corner, bordered by two windows. It would be a perfect spot to read.

Kalan strode toward her waving the condom. Thinking about what came next had her inner walls cramping with need. She wanted him so badly. He tore open the foil and was about to put it on when she stopped him.

He looked up. "What's the matter? Have you changed your mind?"

"No! B…but…" She looked down at his massive cock and licked her lips then brought her lust-filled eyes up to his. "I want to taste you first."

"Goddess help me, but I'm so on the edge, I might blow."

She smiled. "I'll be quick." Then she added a muffled *or not* as she dropped onto the soft carpet. Before he could change his mind, Elana drew his big shaft toward her and encompassed as much of it in her mouth as she could. The problem was that she was only able to fit about two to three inches. While he moaned then planted a hand on her head, she wanted him a sexually frustrated mess before they made love.

With her free hand, she cupped his balls and simultaneously pumped her other fist up and down the rest of his shaft.

Before she could even swipe her tongue back over the head, he grabbed her shoulders and lifted her to her feet. "Enough."

His nails actually grew before her eyes and his teeth elongated. He glanced away. "Sorry. Please, Elana."

Please, what?

Now it was his turn to go down on his knees. Hooking his thumbs in the waistband of her pajama bottoms, he dragged them down, closed his eyes, and inhaled. "So sweet." His reverent tone almost made her believe he was falling in love with her.

She stepped out of them, a bit self-conscious until he opened her folds and lapped up her juices. Then all embarrassment disappeared as bolts of electricity shot straight through her. She swore his tongue was closer to sandpaper than silk, but oh, how that set her whole body on fire. She planted her palms behind her on the wall next to his bedroom door to gain some control, but when he quickly flicked his tongue over her clit then sucked it into his mouth, she lost it. If it hadn't been so long since she'd made love with a man, she might have lasted. Then again, just being with her dream man almost made her come.

When her climax finally ebbed, he sat back on his haunches. She'd been about to apologize when he grinned. "What?" she asked.

"You are beautiful when you soar. I love how responsive you are."

He stood, leaned over, and then kissed her again like a man possessed. Their tongues danced, dueled, and explored—as did her hands. This time she didn't hold back. She grabbed his ass, and when he didn't balk, it boosted her confidence. He had buns of steel, and she could only imagine what kind of power this man could generate. She prayed she could accommodate him.

He broke the kiss and then stared at her, making her a little uncomfortable with the intensity.

Kalan dropped his forehead down to hers and growled. Then suddenly, he spun her around and pressed a hand on her back, forcing her to support herself by palming the wall. Latex snapped and a second later, he widened her legs with his foot.

"You have no idea how much being around you has caused me to lose sleep."

How was that possible? "You barely know me."

"My bear knows he wants you."

She didn't care about his bear. Wanting the man, she craned her neck to look behind her. "I'm about to make love with *you*, not your bear."

"I'm afraid we come as a package, honey, but I don't think you'll be disappointed."

Chapter Thirteen

ELANA HAD BEEN a bit confused when Kalan said his bear half wanted her too, but all thoughts were erased when his fingers plucked both of her nipples. He then pressed his rock hard pecs against her back, and the hair on his chest tickled her skin, despite it being soft.

"I want you to relax and enjoy," he whispered into her ear.

Kalan seemed to understand the perfect combination of tension, pressure, and timing to make her want him even more. His sheathed cock then slid between her legs, and when he rubbed it back and forth across her slit, she became wetter than the flowers after a long rain.

"Oh my God, please!" she begged.

"Please what? You want it slow and easy or hard and fast?"

Both were good but right now, but for their first time, she wanted to feel all his pent up desire slamming against her. "Hard and….oh hell, please just give it to me now!"

He growled. "You asked for it, but know that it will take every ounce of control not to claim you quickly."

Claim her? What did that mean? Was that the same as mating? It was too soon to be thinking about something so permanent—or maybe not. Her body was singing with pleasure so intense that she never wanted to stop.

He lowered one hand and lightly brushed his palm over her belly. Removing his cock from between her legs, he slipped a finger between her folds and into her slippery hole. Sweet Jesus, but that one action had her breath coming out too fast, forcing her to curl her fingers on the wall and lower her head. The urge to press her hips back nearly undid her, but she remained still.

"What you do to me," he panted. From the low, gravelly sound of his voice, he was barely hanging on too.

His finger disappeared from between her legs and was replaced by the head of his cock. This was it. The moment she'd dreamed about for years. The tall, muscular, hunky man slipped one hand up her belly and nabbed her breast, plucking and twisting the tip to the point that almost made her come again. But she wouldn't. She'd wait this time so they could find release together.

The head of his cock found her entrance, and she sucked in a breath, tightening her inner walls.

"I need you to relax and to trust me to know just how much pressure to give you and when. Can you do that?"

Trust a man? Or relax? "I'll try."

Blowing out a breath, Elana concentrated on the bliss bombarding her and forced her mind to stop her incessant questioning. He returned his hands to her breasts and lowered his lips to her shoulder. "You smell so good."

She'd been about to say it was probably the smoke from the campfire, but then she remembered she had showered before going to bed and then had rubbed in some scented cream.

Before she could comment, he pressed her tits together and plunged into her. Stars burst on the back of her lids as her breath whooshed out. Despite being slick inside, his huge cock stretched her to the max, sending sparks of pain mixed with delight in every direction.

"Fuck, honey. You're so tight."

She was tight because he was too damn big, but this time she kept her comment to herself. He withdrew and then forged his way down her channel again. He made it farther this time, and total joy nearly overwhelmed her. Elana hadn't meant to moan, but he'd pushed her past her erotic threshold.

When he nibbled on her shoulder, bursts of pleasure shot down her side straight to her clit, and she couldn't help it but tighten her hold on him. His teeth pressed on her shoulder as if he needed to bite her to gain control. Between his roaming fingers plying her breasts with pleasure, and his slow moving cock, she wanted to scream.

Kalan must have sensed her need, because he grunted, withdrew, and drove into her. Lust, passion, and desire filled her.

He slid his hands to her waist as he refocused his lips on her earlobe, tugging and nibbling on the sensitive shell. That alone was enough to drive her crazy with want. The man seemed to have a second sense about every erotic spot on her body, and if she wasn't careful, she could become addicted to this kind of loving.

Kalan lowered his forehead to her shoulder, tightened his hold on her waist, and pounded into her again, lighting her up from the inside out. Without thinking, she arched her back, which caused her hips to press harder against his.

"You've done it now. I can't stop."

Neither could she.

She wiggled her hips, and he went wild. As he pummeled into her, she met his thrusts with equal power. Every time his cock reached the end, her climax came closer to exploding.

He reached up again, pinched her nipples, and drove into her until she swore he'd come out the other end. She could no longer hold back. The erotic sensations tossed her over the proverbial erotic cliff, and what sounded like a garbled scream erupted from her throat. Seconds later, Kalan's cock pulsed and throbbed as his heated cum filled the condom. Right then and there, Elana realized there would never be another man in her life besides Kalan Murdoch.

He lifted off her back but didn't withdraw. "That had to be the most intense sexual experience I've ever had," he said in several breaths.

Tears of joy brimmed her lashes. "For me too."

Kalan hugged her for a few seconds then withdrew and stepped back. Slowly, Elana straightened.

He turned her around to face. "What do say we shower? Then you're sleeping with me," he said.

Oh, she liked that idea just fine. "I am good with both of those ideas, but do you sleep as a bear?"

He wrapped his arms around her and looked into her eyes. "Not normally but would you feel better if I shifted and slept on the floor?"

"Only if I can pet you and ride on your back again," she said, knowing full well that he'd never go for it.

"Woman, there is definitely going to be some riding going on but we are both going to be in my bed and fully human." In a flash, he had her over his shoulder and did a quick swat to her ass. With both of them laughing he carried her off to the shower.

This had to be the best vacation place in all of Tennessee.

THE NEXT MORNING, Kalan had been awake for half an hour by the time Elana roused. He'd remained in bed and just watched her breathe. She was so beautiful and perfect in every way, but if he wanted to get anything done, he had to leave soon.

While he didn't want to leave her side, especially after being snuggled up against her for the last few hours, finding who'd murdered her parents had to be his number one priority—once he made sure she was safe.

"Hey," she said in a sexy morning voice before he could lift the covers and get up. Elana reached out for his cock, but he stopped her.

"As tempting as you are, if we start anything now, I won't be able to control myself, and I really need to check out a lead in the case." Giving her a soft smile, he ran his fingers across her forehead and then tucked a piece of hair behind her ear.

"A lead?"

"It might be nothing, but I have to check it out. I can't give you any details."

She sighed. "It's just as well you can't stay. I'm not sure I could resist you."

That made him smile. He tapped her nose. "Listen, I texted Dad, and he's going to come over to make sure you stay out of trouble."

"Me, trouble?"

He cocked a brow. "You did go into work when I asked you not to."

"There were extenuating circumstances." She wrinkled her nose. "Didn't you say your dad was really strict?"

Kalan chuckled. "At times, he can be, which is why you need to do as he says."

"I'll be good."

"If he bores you with his stories, just tell him to shut up."

She tapped her chest. "I would never do that. I'm a good girl."

"You weren't a good girl last night." He winked.

She laughed as she waggled her eyebrows at him then pushed up on her elbow. She leaned in and gave him a light sensual kiss, and when he looked into her eyes, the sleepy haze that was there before had disappeared. Her new look screamed danger—like she wanted to devour him. As much as he would have preferred to stay and lose himself in her, he had to go to work.

Kalan gave her another quick kiss as he crawled out of bed and tried to forget the way her tits were exposed and there for the plucking. As he drew on his pants, hair sprouted on his body. Kalan couldn't believe that his attraction to her was even more intense after having made love with her. Here he was hoping it would diminish with more exposure.

Fool.

A knock sounded on his door. Normally, he kept his place unlocked, but he had to secure his home now that Elana was here. "That's Dad. I'll try not to be long," he told her.

With that, he rushed out and opened the door to his father's smiling face "So where is she?" Dad tried to look behind him.

His father was dressed in jeans and a nice button-down shirt. Apparently, he wanted to make a good impression, for which Kalan was glad.

When he'd told his father that Elana was his mate, he thought his father would say it was impossible for a bear shifter to be with a human. Instead, he said it would be an honor to welcome her into the family.

"She's still in bed so be quiet, and for goodness sake, don't tell her about all my stupid mistakes as a kid."

The smile never left his father's face. "Don't you worry. I'll make sure she stays safe."

That was all he could ask. "I'm heading up to Changeling territory, so I'm going to see if Rye will come with me."

"Just be careful. I had to tangle with those sons of bitches a few times in my day. It wasn't pleasant."

He needed to speak with his father about whether he knew anything about the Changelings having more powers—magical ones—but he didn't want to further delay his investigation.

As soon as Kalan left, he mentally contacted Rye. *"You free today to check out the lead I received from James?"* He'd given Rye the brief rundown from yesterday's discussion with the immortal. He'd also shared James's words of wisdom about being there for them merely to provide a nudge.

"I don't have to be at work until five. When do you want to go?"

"Now?"

"Come on over. I'll be ready."

Kalan hopped in his Jeep and drove the few hundred feet to Rye's house where his Alpha was waiting outside. Even if he had been on duty, he bet Rye would have found someone to cover for him at the fire station. Protecting their Clan was his main focus—besides Izzy, of course.

Rye slipped in and closed the door. "You have the address?"

Kalan handed him his phone. "I put it in here. You can navigate with the GPS."

Rye took it. "How do you want to handle this?"

That was the hard part. Changelings could be vicious and uncooperative, or pretend to be your best bud so that you'd basically leave them alone. Another difference was that several lone wolves and bears lived in the same area, so it was impossible to tell which wolf was a Changeling and which one wasn't. If only they could sense a Changeling from a regular shifter, life would be much easier. At least the red moon wouldn't occur for another few weeks, so they were safe from some of their shenanigans for now.

"I plan on telling him we know he tried to buy some sardonyx from the Stanleys, and then ask him where he was the night of their murder," Kalan said.

"The best we can hope for is to catch the guilt in his eyes. If he runs, between the two of us, we can take him."

"I'm not here to kill him." Sometimes his Alpha didn't think about the consequences. When Rye had killed the Changeling from Scotland, Kalan had broken more laws than he'd wanted to think about covering Rye's ass. Doing so again, might be harder to hide.

Rye shrugged. "I guess you'd have to clean up the mess if we do."

Some things would never change. "Too true."

After a wrong turn, they located the address. Up in the hills, the signal cut in and out, making the GPS unreliable. Kalan parked at the end of the driveway to stay hidden from sight of the house and for a quick escape should they need it. They both exited the car, and from the way Rye was glancing around, he was trying to detect other shifters and potential traps.

"I'm not sensing anyone here," Kalan said.

Rye glanced over at him. "It's early. He could be at work."

Because Changelings caused so much trouble in Silver Lake, it was hard to think of them as having integrated themselves so seamlessly into the human world. "I say we knock anyway."

"I'll go around back," Rye telepathed.

The house was a one-story clapboard style home in disrepair. He knocked. "Chris Darden?"

Kalan had been smart enough to wear his civilian clothes. A uniformed cop in the mountains was asking for trouble. He waited a beat but when he received no answer, he knocked again.

"You see anything?" he telepathed Rye.

"Ah, Kalan, I think you need to come here."

From the serious tone, it wasn't good. Kalan rushed around to the back of the house. "What is it?"

"Look inside."

Kalan pressed his way through the hedge and peered into the window. "Well, fuck."

A man, who he assumed was Darden, lay dead on the kitchen floor. Some of the kitchen chairs were knocked over or out of place, implying the fight had been rather violent. The fact he was naked indicated he might have been in his shifted form when he died, and the gash on his throat said another werewolf had ended his life.

The delicate part of dealing with a Changeling death was explaining to a human how a man inside his own house would have his throat ripped out by a wolf. Yup, Kalan might have to leave the body for the Changelings to deal with.

"You want to check inside?" Rye asked. "You said James told you the man was supposed to buy some sardonyx from the Stanleys. It's possible whoever killed Darden killed the Stanleys."

"The murderer might have believed Darden received the sardonyx, and he wanted it for himself."

"Could be." Rye pulled on a pair of rubber gloves and jiggled the handle to the back door. Kalan was pleased he'd listened to his many warnings about leaving no trace and did the same.

To his surprise, the back door was open. "That was lucky, or else the killer was careless. We need to be sure not disturb anything."

Rye speared him with a glance. "Sometimes I think you having a job on the force does more harm than good for me."

He and Rye had been round and round about his desire to follow the law. "It helps more than it hurts."

"Maybe, and by the way, where's your weapon?"

"In my glove compartment. I'm not carrying because I didn't want him to figure out I'm a deputy." Rye shrugged and stepped inside. Kalan followed and inhaled, detecting the usual stench of death. "From the lack of bloating, it doesn't like he's been dead for long."

"I'll look around the living room," Rye said.

"You have any idea what you're looking for?"

"Nope." Rye disappeared around the corner while Kalan searched some the other rooms.

The doors on the wooden kitchen cabinets were half off their hinges and the linoleum had several burn marks on it. The kitchen table was metal with a Formica top that looked as if it hadn't been cleaned in ages.

The search of the two bedrooms and one bathroom didn't take long nor did it provide him with anything useful. Rye called to him. "Come here."

"What did you find?"

"See for yourself."

Sometimes Rye was too dramatic for Kalan's tastes. "Coming."

Chapter Fourteen

ELANA WASN'T ABOUT to stay in bed with Kalan's father in the other room, so she slid out from under the covers and quickly dressed. The only conservative top she had was the long sleeve shirt she'd worn last night, and that still smelled of smoke from their cookout, which meant she'd have to go with the T-shirt with a pink rose on it. It had a hole in the sleeve, but the other ones she'd packed were too risqué. Thankfully, in her befuddled state, she'd actually grabbed some jeans without the rips in them.

Even though she was in the customer service business, she wasn't sure what to say to his dad. *Hi, Mr. Murdoch, sorry I was still in bed when you arrived. Your son spent the night boffing me into another dimension.* Ah, no. Kalan probably told him she was here only because she needed his protection.

Here goes. She stepped into the living room. "Hello."

An older version of Kalan looked up, whipped off his glasses, and stuffed them in his shirt pocket. He then jumped up. Oh, my, he was even taller and bigger than Kalan—though not as muscular—but didn't look a day over sixty.

"You must be Elana."

"Yes and you must be Kalan's dad." She reached out and shook his hand. "I appreciate you taking the time to watch over me, Mr. Murdoch."

He waved a hand. "Nonsense. It makes me feel useful. You want some breakfast? My son never really learned how to cook, but I'm quite good."

Clearly, Kalan had inherited his self-confidence from his dad. Mr. Murdoch wasn't being all that fair to his son though. Kalan's hot dogs had been cooked to perfection. "I'd love some."

She followed Kalan's dad to the kitchen and sat down on one of the padded stools at the island. He yanked some food from the fridge as if he'd been in this kitchen many times. "How do you like your eggs?"

"Scrambled is good."

He retrieved a metal bowl from under the island and set half a dozen eggs next to it.

"Coffee's ready if you want some," he said.

"Thanks." Elana poured a cup then returned to her seat. She wasn't sure what topics were appropriate, but dads always liked to talk about their kids.

"Kalan said he cut up a lot in school."

"He told you that?" She nodded. "It was just teenage stuff. I bet Kalan didn't tell you about all the good things he did."

"No." *We were too busy tearing off each other's clothes.*

"Mind you, my boy could be a devil, but he always had a kind heart."

She leaned on the counter, interested in hearing details about Kalan's life. "Do tell."

Mr. Murdoch glanced at the ceiling. "When Kalan was around ten, he and his friends believed it was their job to protect the neighborhood. Guess it was because I was in the security business myself, and Kalan always wanted to do what I did—up to a point. Anyway, each night they'd ride around the streets carrying pads of paper, jotting down anything that looked out of the ordinary."

She could picture Kalan doing that. "What did they take note of?"

"If a window was broken or some family had too many newspapers out front. Much to their disappointment, homes around Silver Lake didn't have much crime, so that's why they had to settle for small disturbances."

That was cute. "What was Kalan like as a kid when he was home?"

Mr. Murdoch cracked open the eggs and then tossed the shells in the sink. "Let's just say he didn't take many things seriously. He believed the purpose of life was to have fun. He has changed, though. Believe it or not, it took pulling teeth to get him to clean his room." Mr. Murdoch waved a hand. "Look at him now. He's a neat freak."

She'd seen Kalan's happy-go-lucky attitude, but he had his serious side too. From what Mr. Murdoch said, Kalan was just a normal, well-adjusted boy—who happened to be a bear shifter. She wanted to ask how old Kalan was when he first shifted, how strong he was as a kid, and because he was a bear, did he like fish more than meat, but she didn't know Mr. Murdoch well enough to ask. He might be upset if he thought she was obsessed with his son.

"Tell me a bit about yourself," Mr. Murdoch said after he whipped up the eggs, added some milk, and then poured the mixture into the now heated pan. "By the way, I'm very sorry to hear about your parents. Terrible tragedy."

"Thank you. Did you know them?"

"I knew their names and who they were, but we'd never spoken."

"I'm not surprised. They weren't around much." Under her breath, she mumbled, *even for my childhood*. Elana looked up to see if he heard the last part, but Mr. Murdoch had looked away. In a hurry to change the conversation to something happier, she blurted out, "I own my own flower shop."

He smiled. "Kalan told me. What do like the best about being an entrepreneur?"

That was easy. "While I'm able to decide what to buy and what prices to charge, the best part is being able to make people happy with my arrangements. I love being creative."

He smiled, and she could see a lot of his son in him—the same eyes, straight nose and cute dimples.

"You and Kalan seem like a perfect match."

Her heart nearly stopped at his comment. They weren't even dating. Having wild, intensely crazy sex one time didn't mean they were a couple. "Pardon me?"

"Kalan always had this bad boy image and never seemed willing to give his heart to any girl. You seem to be helping him change all that."

She didn't dare hope that was true. "Perhaps it's because his job is to protect me that he has to take things more seriously."

"I don't think so. I know my son." His dad stirred the eggs in the pan. "I like you. You're direct and seem like a sensible girl. While the circumstances aren't the best, I'm glad Kalan was assigned to protect you."

"Me, too."

"WHAT DID YOU find?" Kalan asked as he entered Darden's living room.

Rye held up a piece of paper. "The Stanley's address was rolled up in a newspaper."

"Well, well. That is interesting. I guess James's intel was spot on. This implies Darden either planned to see the Stanleys about the purchase or he'd already visited them. But did he kill them?"

Rye placed a hip on the desk. "We could come up with a dozen scenarios, all plausible, but without further evidence, we basically have squat."

"It's better than nothing. My question is why was he hiding the address? Seems to me he'd want to ditch it once he visited them—assuming he already had."

"True. If Darden murdered the Stanleys, why is he dead?" Rye asked.

"Excellent question." One he'd yet to figure out. "We need more evidence if we have any chance of connecting him to the murders."

Rye held up a hand. "A car's coming up the drive."

That wasn't good. The person would know someone was there

since his Jeep was on the street next to the drive. Kalan had never tested the front door to see if it was unlocked, but there wasn't time now. He doubted it was the killer since there would be no good reason to kill Darden and then return so soon after—unless he'd left something behind that would incriminate him.

The vehicle came to a stop in front of the house, and Kalan detected a wolf signature. "Let's head to the back."

They rushed through the living room to the kitchen and stepped past the dead body. Kalan didn't want to go outside in case the person planned to use the back entrance. There was a room off the kitchen, which might afford a place to hide, but before they could decide where to go, the front door opened. They pressed their backs against a wall to avoid immediate detection, but this person surely had to recognize the two shifter signatures.

"Hey, Chris, where are you, man? Spotted a car at the end of the driveway. Who's here?"

The two shifter signatures wouldn't raise a red flag since the man would assume one was Chris and the other a visitor. Drawers opened and slammed shut. Curses followed.

"It's time to see what he's up to," Kalan telepathed.

Both he and Rye strutted out to the living room and found the man with his hand in the desk drawer. He whipped around and froze. The intruder was of average size and in need of a shave and a haircut. Glancing right then left, he turned then charged outside.

"Fuck," Rye said.

They both took off after him. The skinny man didn't have a prayer. Before the guy had the chance to shift, Kalan nabbed him by the back of his shirt. The intruder twisted around and managed one swing before Rye grabbed his hands and tugged them behind his back.

"Got any cuffs?" Rye asked.

"As a matter of fact I do." Kalan grinned, slipped the pair from his back pocket, and tossed them to Rye. Kalan leveled a stare at the man. "Don't even think about running or shifting. Bears like to eat wolves for lunch."

"I'd like to see you try."

"Don't tempt me." Kalan might have shifted just to scare the guy, but he didn't have a spare outfit in the Jeep.

The newcomer lifted his chin. "I didn't do anything."

"Let's get you inside where we can chat about whether that's fact or fiction."

The man jerked away from Rye but thankfully followed Kalan inside. From the kitchen, Kalan snatched a chair and brought it to the living room. "Sit."

He spit but then obeyed. "I ain't telling you goons jack shit."

Kalan shrugged. He'd dealt with guys like many times this before. They thought they were tough until things went south. Then they sang like a canary. "Why not, if you haven't done anything wrong?"

"There are some people around here who wouldn't appreciate me talking, that's why."

"Just tell us why you're here then."

"I was looking for something I gave Chris. I guess he's not here, but he should arrive any minute. He'll explain everything."

From his arrogance, he truly believed his friend was still alive. "Come with me."

Rye helped the cuffed man stand then shoved him forward. The guy grunted. A few steps later, he was staring into the dead eyes of Chris Darden. "Holy fuck." He spun around and looked like he was about to shit. "You fuckers. Why did you kill him?"

Kalan was about to say that they hadn't, but then thought better of it. "Because he wouldn't tell us what we wanted to know."

"Okay, okay. It was an address. I was looking for a fucking address. There's no crime in that."

Rye slipped the piece of paper from his pocket. "This the one you want?"

The man squinted. "Yeah." He reached out to take it, only to realize he was cuffed. Rye shoved the piece of paper back in his pocket. "That's mine. Give it back."

The intruder acted like he was still in high school. Kalan dragged him back to the living room and sat him down. "Tell me what you know about the Stanleys."

"Never heard of them."

As much as Kalan wanted to smack him, he feared it would make the man clam up faster. "The address you claimed belonged to you has their name on it."

"Oh. I forgot."

Kalan was losing his patience. "Why did you need to see them?"

"I ordered something from them, but then they fucking tried to cheat me."

Okay, Kalan hadn't expected that. "Be more specific."

He pressed his lips together. "Rye, convince him," Kalan said.

Rye clasped the man's neck and began to squeeze. "Shift and I'll tear your throat out before you reach the door." Rye's harsh tone convinced Kalan his Alpha might do as he threatened. This Changeling would be a fool not to believe him.

"Fine."

Rye let go. "Me and Chris were supposed to buy some sardonyx from the Stanleys. They're importers."

That much he'd already figured out—with help from James. "Had you purchased this stone from them before?"

"Yes, only this time that ass, Mr. Stanley, asked for more money. Said it was harder to get this time."

"What did you do?"

He glanced to the kitchen. "It wasn't what I did, it was what Chris did. He went at the man and stabbed him in the gut. The ass deserved it too."

That was consistent with their injuries. "Where was Mrs. Stanley at the time?"

"Bitch comes out from the kitchen and starts screaming at us for harming her SOB husband. She acted like we were the ones who'd done something wrong."

"You shut her up?" Rye asked slapping him in the back of the head.

"No, motherfucker. Chris got her. In the gut, just like her old man."

Kalan would have to see if forensics could prove one knife stabbed both people or if this dude had taken things into his own hands. Kalan jerked him to his feet. "You're coming with us."

"I ain't going anywhere with you two."

"Do you really think you have a choice?"

The dude lifted his chin. "You can't keep my kind in jail. I'll just touch someone and then blend in."

He was right. "Can't do that for another few weeks, though." That was when another red moon would occur. Rye dragged him out.

"What are you going to do with Chris?" the man asked, almost acting as if he cared.

"I'm sure your kind will come looking for him eventually."

"As soon as I'm out of your stupid jail, I'm telling them you did it."

Them? He wanted to ask if he was referring to the Changeling Council, but this man had no reason to answer.

Rye just shook his head. After securing the smug asshole in the back of Kalan's Jeep, Kalan stepped away from his vehicle and called his brother Jackson who worked with Rye's brother at McKinnon and Associates.

"Hey, what's up?" Jackson asked.

"I need a big favor." When they brought this man into the station, most likely he'd say that he and Rye had killed his friend. Should that happened, Kalan wanted no evidence of the man. It would mean Chris's murderer would get away with the crime, but that couldn't be helped. He and Rye didn't need to be dragged through a long, drawn out trial.

Kalan spent a few minutes explaining what happened and then gave Jackson the address.

"Don't worry about a thing. Your little brother has your back. But you owe me."

"Big time, but be quick. When someone from the station heads on up here, we don't need them to find the body."

"Can do."

Kalan glanced upward. He couldn't imagine what it would take to pay off that debt. Once he was satisfied Jackson would take care of the body, he jumped into the driver's seat and relayed to Rye his conversation with his brother.

Smart move, Rye telephathed.

Kalan drove straight to the sheriff's department where he escorted the interloper directly to central booking.

"What is he being charged with?" the booking officer asked.

"Accessory to murder."

The man's eyes widened. "That's bullshit. I told you I had nothing to do with their deaths."

"But you were there, which makes you an accessory."

He pointed to both Kalan and Rye. "I might have witnessed a murder, but these two killed my friend."

Kalan put on his best acting face. "What are you talking about?"

"You killed Chris Darden."

"I have no idea who that is."

"What's your name," the officer asked.

The Changeling grunted. "Hank Melton." He argued a bit more about being innocent, but when he got nowhere, he let the officer escort him to a holding cell. Kalan had no doubt the department would send someone to investigate, but they wouldn't find much. Jackson was that good.

Hank Melton, if that was his real name, deserved to spend the rest of his life in jail. He'd shown no remorse about the Stanleys' deaths. Then again, he was a Changeling.

As he and Rye exited the station, Rye turned to him. "You believe Melton? That it was Darden who did the killing?"

"No reason not to, but something seems off. If only the two of them were involved, why is this dude still standing? Why not kill both him and Darden?"

"Maybe they couldn't find him. The Changeling Council could have believed Darden and Melton had the sardonyx. When they didn't deliver it right away, they killed Darden. Melton might have been next."

"That seems plausible. Someone besides Melton is behind this. This guy is too wimpy to have orchestrated the deal."

"I agree. With Darden dead and Melton not talking, I don't know how you're going to find who ordered the buy." Rye pulled open the passenger side door and slid in.

"Tell me about it. I'd ask James, but he doesn't seem willing to give up the info."

"Have you ever tried using Deanna Landon, the psychic, at any of your crime scenes?" Rye asked.

Kalan jammed the key in the ignition and fired up the engine. "Not personally, but the department has. Why?"

"Izzy mentioned that Deanna can often sense how many people were in a room during the time of the murders or theft. Their auras float around for a while she said. Izzy claimed Deanna's been known to recreate scenes with exceptional accuracy."

"Forensics finished at the house yesterday. I'll see if Deanna's free."

Right now, he wanted to forget all about the Changelings and focus on something positive—like nibbling on something or rather someone.

"So how are you and Elana doing?" Rye asked.

"What?" He didn't need to be discussing this with his Alpha—or rather he wasn't ready to.

"I can sense your turmoil."

No use hiding it. "Fine. She distracts me beyond reason." Rye said nothing. "Okay, Elana is my mate. There, are you happy now?"

He glanced over at Rye, who was grinning. "Totally."

Chapter Fifteen

After Kalan dropped Rye off at his house, he hurried back to Elana, wanting, or rather needing to celebrate with her. His biggest hurdle now would be to convince his dad to go home. Having his father hang out and talk shop would only make his desire to be alone with his mate that much stronger.

Hank Melton had admitted that Chris had murdered Elana's parents, so the hard court press to insulate her from all the danger was now gone. He couldn't dismiss the fact that someone had killed Darden, however. Not that Kalan gave a shit about the Changeling's death, but he wished he understood whether this new killer was still focused on finding the sardonyx. If so, would he believe Elana had it, and would she therefore still be in danger?

None of the crime scene investigators had reported finding a large sum of money at the Stanley home, so it appeared the killers hadn't paid for the goods yet—unless the Changelings had set up something in advance, and Elana's parents had tried to double-cross them.

Despite being able to provide some closure for Elana, Kalan wasn't looking forward to telling her that her parents probably hadn't given her that stone because it reminded them of her good heart. Instead, they'd given her the so-called gift so they could honestly tell Darden and Melton they didn't have it on them. The fact the killers tore up the Stanley mansion, Elana's apartment, and Brian's hotel room implied the men weren't going to stop until they located it. He could only hope those two who'd trashed Elana's apartment and Brian's room were now dead or in custody.

Kalan pulled into his driveway, his mind suddenly jolted by the most obvious fact of all. Why would these men have gone to Brian's hotel room? They wouldn't have known the Stanleys even had a son unless they'd met him. *Fuck.* Brian might be involved after all. Until he figured out how, he wouldn't tell Elana about his concern.

What he needed right now was to forget his troubles by delving into Elana's sweetness. He'd deal with those unanswered questions later.

As soon as he eased out of his Jeep, his senses shot to high alert. The number of family shifter signatures overwhelmed him, as did the noise coming from the backyard. What the hell was going on? Elana's laugh floated toward him, creating more confusion.

Because it was faster to go through the house to reach them than by going around to the back, he charged toward the front door. Kalan stepped inside and stopped, not believing his eyes. Everyone was sitting on the porch, jammed together at the table filled with snacks of all kinds. His dad, mom, and Blair, as well as two members from Rye's family, Finn and Chelsea were there. He'd asked his father to watch Elana for a few hours, not invite his whole damn family to a party.

Kalan was about to barge in and demand answers when his dad stood and lifted a red Solo cup, as if he was about to toast something. At that moment, Kalan wished he had the ability to become invisible.

"To Kalan's mate!" His dad smiled down on Elana.

His mate? He told her? Holy crap. If it wouldn't upset his mother, he'd kill his father right now. Yes, Elana was his mate, but he'd wanted to take his time to establish a long and trusting relationship before he told her.

"Thank you," she said with the sweetest of smiles.

Thank you? It was only last night that she'd learned werebears even existed, yet she was okay with being a mate? Most likely Izzy had filled her in on what happened in the process, but that didn't excuse his father's comment.

His dad sat down. "Has he bitten you yet?" he asked.

That was it. The man would die a slow and painful death for asking.

"Where? On my ass?"

His siblings laughed at her sassy response.

This was becoming worse by the minute, but Kalan could barely breathe, let alone move. It was as if some witch had put a curse on him. He rubbed the back of his neck and stretched it from side to side, trying to relief the tension that had seeped in.

His mother placed a hand on Elana's arm. *Shit.* He'd seen that look when he was young, and she'd had to explain the facts of life to him. "No, dear. On the neck."

Elana's chin tucked under. "Why would he bite me on the neck? I wouldn't want him to do that. It would hurt."

Izzy must not have provided all the ins and outs of being mated to a shifter.

"It doesn't really hurt, not when you're in the throes of passion." His mother glanced over at Dad and smiled. *Oh you have got to be kidding me. Just kill me now.*

Kalan groaned, but apparently the whole tribe was so engrossed in the discussion that they hadn't even sensed he was there.

"But why?" she asked.

Mom, please just lie.

"You and Kalan are destined for one another. Once he bites you, should you choose to stay with him, your fate will be sealed," his mom explained. "You will be together forever."

"Not to mention you'll be able to shift once the white moon appears," Finn added with way too much enthusiasm.

Kalan pressed his back against the front door, not sure what he should do. It didn't matter that he wanted Elana more than life itself. It was his responsibility to tell her what would happen when they mated. Now, she'd expect him to bite her right away.

He was about to stop this nonsense until he heard Elana squeal in delight. "Are you saying I'll be able to turn into a bear?"

Okay, it was time to put an end to this. He strode out to the large wooden deck.

"Hey, there he is," his dad said. "How did everything go?"

Stay calm and don't kill anyone. To his surprise, being close to Elana allowed him to remain civil. "We found the two men who killed Elana's parents."

She jumped up and threw herself in his arms. "Thank you."

Her hug was so strong he never wanted to move. Over her shoulder, he gave his father the evil eye. It was times like this that he wished he could communicate telepathically with his family and tell them to get the hell out of his home because he had some loving to do—after he put a hurt on every one of the conspirators.

"That's great, son. Who was it?"

"Two men who live in the hills." That should clue him in they were Changelings. Hopefully, his dad had enough sense not to ask questions in front of a human.

"Nice." His dad stood as if to leave. "I gotta tell you, you have an awesome young lady here."

If Kalan said it was too soon to celebrate any kind of mating, it would hurt Elana's feelings. "I know."

His sister pushed back her chair and came over to them. "It's so nice to be around someone who's open to learning new ways of doing things."

Kalan didn't even want to ask what that meant. "Listen, Elana and I have some things to discuss. I appreciate you all keeping her company though."

His mother smiled. "We get the hint. We're leaving. Make sure you bring Elana around soon." Mom hugged both of them.

It seemed to take the group forever to clean up and leave. When he and Elana were finally alone, his aggravation had amped up his desire. As soon as he shut the door, he faced Elana, ready for a million questions. He never expected the huge grin on her face.

"Oh my God. You are the luckiest person alive," she said. "What

I would have given to have such an awesome family. Don't get me wrong, Izzy is like a sister to me, as is Missy, but her parents, especially her dad, can be rather straight-laced."

So could his parents, but he wouldn't mention that now. He stepped toward her and she backed up. "I'm glad you liked them."

Now that they were alone, his bear was tired of being pent up and made it very clear that Kalan needed to make love with her. As in now.

"I more than liked them," she said. "Your sister suggested some exercises I could do when my back starts hurting. She even said I could come into her physical therapy clinic—for free."

He tried to close the gap, but Elana took a step back. Why, he didn't know. "Blair is nice like that."

"And Finn was a hoot." Her back hit the front door.

Keep going. She's only stalling, but she wants you, his bear informed him.

His family had their strengths and weaknesses, but he had other things on his mind than talking about them. "I need to discuss something with you."

Her eyes lit up. "About this mating stuff? Your mom explained some or most of it to me. Finn said that I could learn to shift too. I can't wait until I can run around like a bear."

Her intense excitement was so cute. He bracketed his hands around her head and leaned in close. "Actually, our women shift into muskrats."

Kalan had no idea why he told her that, but he was curious how open minded she really was. When her brows pinched and her lip curled, he worked hard not to laugh.

"A muskrat? My super power will be to turn into a wet, furry rodent?"

He could see the sparkle in her eyes and the crease at the edge of her mouth where she was trying not to smile. She was playing him, the little minx. Goddess how he loved that she gave as good as she got. They would have so much fun together. So, with that thought, he looked her dead in the eyes. "Absolutely. You'll look so cute too. I will just have to make sure not to accidentally sit on you when we've shifted."

"Oh, you will pay for that, Mister." With a laugh, Elana shoved his chest, but her force was so weak, he didn't even move.

Kalan was grinning like a fool. "That all you got, tough girl?" So as not to crowd her, he stepped back and held up his hands pretending to box.

He was thankful she didn't focus on the questionable mating part. He didn't need to be explaining that if they mated right now their attraction would intensify. Until this case concluded, he didn't dare become more distracted than he already was.

"I'll show you tough. Drop your pants and we'll see how strong you are." She nodded to his groin.

Where had this feistiness come from? Was it his family telling her how great she was that had caused it, or the fact her parents' murderers had been caught? Regardless of the origin, he liked her new attitude. A lot.

Not one to turn down a dare, he shucked off his shoes and kicked them aside. "I hope you're ready for the consequences of your actions."

She lifted her chin and this time moved toward him. "Consequences? As in you'll stop me in about thirty seconds once I start sucking on your cock and then lick me until I scream your name?"

Man, did she knew how to turn him on or what? "If you aren't careful, I might shift on you."

"I dare you."

The woman had a good comeback for everything. "How about you do a little strip tease for me and see if you can excite me enough to force a shift?" *Fuck me, if she does that I will be in her so fast it will be over before it starts.* "No, wait. I want to strip *you* first."

"You think your bear can control himself?" She slipped under his arm and then turned to face him.

Shit, she was right, but either way, he was going to have her.

"No, but it sure is going to be fun trying."

She backed up and stepped into the hallway. As he approached her, he unbuttoned his jeans and took them off. Thinking he might need to shift when he headed into Changeling territory, he'd worn as little as possible, which meant he'd gone commando.

Her eyes widened. "Whoa. You do move fast."

"Forgot my briefs."

She glanced to his jeans on the floor. "So I see." Elana edged closer. "Is that stubble new growth?" She dragged a hand down his cheek and his inner bear growled, begging for freedom.

"Could be. If you really want to turn me on, let me take a better look at what you have to offer." He lifted the T-shirt over her head, and the moment he spotted the pink bra, his dick turned harder than the Oak in the backyard. "You're a real temptation."

"So what are you going to do about it?"

He couldn't remember a woman who seemed so at ease with her sexuality, though if anyone had asked if it was possible coming from Elana, he'd have said no. She had implied she hadn't had a full love life. Had their lovemaking caused the change, or had one of Izzy's witch friends put a spell on his woman? It didn't matter. He liked this new version of Elana Stanley.

She'd asked a question. "This."

He cupped her tits and devoured her mouth. When she latched onto his shoulders and invited him in, all thoughts of his parents invading his home disappeared. All he wanted to do was possess her. He explored the roof of her mouth, bumping into her tongue doing the same thing to him. They were tentative at first, but as their breaths entwined, their speed increased.

He finally had to pull away. If he hadn't, he might have done something both of them would have regretted. Elana slipped her hands under his shirt and took it off. Her delicate touch had his senses reeling. The final straw was when she licked her lips, he could no longer resist her.

Kalan backed her up deep into the hallway to make sure no one could see them through the front window. He dropped to his knees and undid the top of her pants then tugged them down. She then toed off her sandals, and as soon as she stepped out of her jeans, he pressed his face against her silky panties. Her womanly scent made it hard to concentrate, especially when he clutched her ass, squeezing her full, round butt. "You turn me on like no one ever has."

"Is that you or your bear talking?"

He looked up at her, his eyelids heavy. "Would it be bad if I said both?"

She grinned and grabbed a hunk of his hair. "Not as long as you hurry."

From her breathy pants, coupled with the scent of her arousal, it wouldn't take long to bring this beauty to climax. Kalan lowered her panties, revealing an reddish brown pot of gold. When she arched her back and widened her stance, he smiled. So sensitive. So alluring. *So mine.*

Had it not been for his bones cracking, he would have spent a long time touching and enjoying her, but since his inner animal was urging him to love her hard and fast, Kalan had no choice but to bare it all. Once he removed her panties, he tossed them aside.

"I'm gonna feast on you today," he said.

"I thought I was getting the first crack at you."

Her words speared him with lust. "I changed my mind."

The first lick tasted like pure nectar and he had to take care not to let his incisors grow. It was bad enough that the hair on his face was thickening. This tasty woman was messing with every hormone in his body, and he wasn't sure he could give her enough satisfaction before he blew.

Clutching her thighs, he buried his face between her legs and flicked her clit back and forth. The grip on his hair increased, and then so did the speed of his tongue. The problem was that her moans and little whimpers were as exciting as if she were devouring his dick. Each swipe of his tongue brought him closer to tossing her on the floor and plunging into her.

"Kalan, yes. More."

His sweet woman was so needy that he intended to give her everything she desired. He licked and sucked her pussy until he could no longer stop himself from sinking his cock into her.

Kalan stood, swept her into his arms and carried her to his bed, before lowering her onto her back. He leaned over and sucked on her tits, his cock awaiting the right moment to take her.

Chapter Sixteen

BEING WITH KALAN exceeded Elana's every expectation. Each lick, tug, and twirl sent her reeling to a place she'd never been before. If only she had ten more sets of arms she could touch every inch of his sensual, muscular body.

"Take me," she huffed.

Kalan growled, and when he plucked her other nipple, sparks of pleasure swirled and dove right between her legs. She planted her feet on the mattress and lifted her hips, hoping to entice him, but all that did was merely press the tip of his cock against her opening. She thought he would enter her right away, but he didn't. The man seemed determined to torture her.

As if he could read her mind, he lifted his head and kissed her. Needing to turn him on even more, she reached between them and grabbed his hard shaft.

Kalan broke the kiss, growled, and slipped out of her grasp. He then plunged into her. Holy balls of fire. His girth, along with the friction, ignited every nerve ending and caused bolts of electricity to sizzle inside her. To keep from flying apart at the seams, she had to dig her nails into his hips and hold on for dear life.

Thrust for thrust, she met his driving force. He then lowered his head and kissed her neck. Was this it? More than anything, she wanted him to bite her to complete the mating process, but she wouldn't beg. He needed to decide when the timing was right.

"I'm so damn close," he said, his voice so low she barely heard the words.

"Me, too."

"Then let go Elana, and I'll catch you."

His grip tightened, and with each stroke, her climax built. Needing it all, she wrapped her legs around his waist, dropped her head back, and let every erotic sensation wash over her. On the next thrust, her climax claimed her. Colors flashed before her eyes, and she felt like she was outside of her body. Never before had she experienced anything so intense.

"Need you so much," Kalan said, the growl evident in his voice as his hot seed spilled into her.

Kalan's heavy body then pressed down on her and held her as if he never wanted to let her go. After their breathing evened out, he slid out. "Be right back."

He returned moments later and wiped her clean. When she sat up, she pointed to a wet spot on the sheets. "Missed a bit."

His eyes widened, and then he wiped up the mess. "Fuck. I forgot a condom. I'm so sorry. I got carried away."

"That's okay. I'm on the pill."

He blew out a breath. "One can't be too careful."

As happy as she was that he wanted to be responsible, she could also envision having Kalan's child—assuming she could take the baby to work or have someone watch him or her during the day. She'd always made a promise that she would never abandon a child.

Don't even go there. Kalan hadn't tried to bite her, which meant he wasn't ready to be mated—assuming this whole fated thing was for real. Izzy thought it was, but maybe that only worked with wolf shifters.

Elana eased off the bed and gathered her pajamas, trying hard to not let the tear that was teetering on her lid fall. She'd seen the desire in his eyes, but somehow, he wasn't ready to be with her.

Needing some time to think, she decided it would be best to distance herself from her desires—assuming she could. The fastest way to douse her ongoing urges would be find out more about her parents' deaths. That was sure to be a mood killer.

Kalan followed her into the living room where he finished dressing. "Did these men say why they murdered my parents?" she asked.

Kalan's eyes widened, probably wondering how she could go from loving to analytical in a heartbeat. He sat on the sofa's chair arm and motioned for her to sit on the seat next to him. At first she debated sitting across from him, but she wasn't ready to for that much distance.

"No, but I did receive a tip about a man by the name of Chris Darden who might have been responsible for your parents' deaths. However, when Rye and I arrived at his house, he was dead."

More deaths? If her insides hadn't been rubbed numb by Kalan's recent action, she might have experienced more horror. "Guess he's not talking. Do you know who killed him?"

"No." Kalan explained that while he and Rye were there, a man came looking for the address to her parents' home. Most likely, he didn't want the evidence lying about.

"Do you think he killed this Chris guy?"

"No, but the next question is, who did?"

From the way he kept looking off to the side, he wasn't telling her something. "What is it? And be straight with me, please."

Kalan blew out a breath. "Mind you this comes from a man who was an accomplice to murder, if not the murderer himself, but he said he'd offered to buy what appeared to be the piece of sardonyx your parents gave you."

She sank back against the sofa. "They were murdered over a piece of stone?"

"Seems so."

"It's that valuable?"

"I wish I knew, though Izzy might be able to shed some light on the power of crystals and rocks."

Nothing was making sense. "Why give it to me if they already had a buyer for it?" His lips pressed into a thin line. That wasn't good. "Unless they'd brought back two pieces."

Kalan shifted uncomfortably on the arm. "That I don't know. According to the second man, Hank Melton, your parents claimed they didn't have any of the stone, but that they could get it. They were trying to raise the price. Rye and I think they gave it to you for safe keeping."

Her stomach cramped as waves of lost hope washed over her. "I guess leopards don't change their spots after all. I can't believe they were planning to ask for it back."

Kalan shrugged. "We'll never know."

"So now what happens?"

He motioned for her to scoot over and then he slid down onto the spot she'd just vacated. "I know you want to resume your life, and I can't blame you, but your apartment needs a bit more work. Do you mind staying here until then?" He picked up her hand and kissed her knuckles.

How his touch could twist her insides so soon after the explosive sex, she didn't know. "Okay, thank you, but is it safe to go back to work?" A killer, who might something she had, was on the loose.

He stroked her cheek. "Yes, but you'll need to be careful."

"I will. I understand that whoever wanted to buy the stone could still want it."

He nodded. "Which leads me to ask if you'd be willing to leave the stone in the safe?"

"I have no emotional attachment to it anymore, especially now that it hadn't really been a gift from my parents."

Kalan's shoulders visibly relaxed. "I'll ask Dad to keep an eye on you while you're at the shop."

Her initial reaction was to say no, but in light of the recent circumstances, she'd welcome the added protection. "I'm good with that."

"Thank you. I'll call him. Then I need to set up a reading by Deanna Landon at your parents' house."

She'd met Deanna, but didn't understand why he'd need a reading. "Have you used her before?"

He rubbed her arm. "Not personally, but her psychic abilities have helped in other cases."

That was pretty cool. "I thought you said the case was closed since you found the murderers."

"As far as the police are concerned it is closed. But there is still the murder of that Darden fellow."

That made sense. "Hence the reason why your father will be my invisible bodyguard and why you want to see if Darden's killer might have been in the house, right?"

"You're a smart one."

"Given you came here directly after arresting that man, I'm guessing you haven't told Brian anything about capturing the killers?"

He dragged a hand down his jaw. "Not yet. There are a few things that aren't fitting neatly into place."

She didn't like the sound of that. "You don't believe Brian was in on it, do you?"

"No, but I think somehow he might have unknowingly seen who they were right before the home invasion," he said, expressing his concern.

"If I didn't know Brian was my brother, how would they have figured it out, unless my parents told the killers?"

Kalan snapped his fingers. "Your brother said company arrived at your parents' house that first night, which was why he left before he was finished speaking with them. That company might have been Darden and Melton."

"Only one way to find out," she said.

"Ask him. Trust me, I intend to."

As curious as Elana was about Brian, she was still thinking about what to say to him. Maybe after Kalan had his spoke with her brother, she'd ask to see him too.

After dinner, Elana insisted she clean up, so Kalan ducked into the bedroom and called his dad to ask if he could help keep an eye on his mate—or rather his soon-to-be mate.

"Are you still expecting trouble? I though you said you caught those two Changelings?"

Kalan had not specifically said who they were, but the assumption was valid. He went through the series of events and how someone had killed Darden. "I'm thinking this killer might have been planning to kill Melton before he did something stupid, only we got to him first."

"That sounds reasonable. You're right to be careful. I'll make sure no one gets near Elana. You can count on me."

"I wasn't able to count on you to keep your mouth shut about Elana being my chosen mate. What were you thinking?" Once the words were out, he realized this call might have been an excuse to chastise his dad.

The long silence told him volumes. "I don't keep anything from your mother. If she ever found out I knew something and didn't tell her....let's just say I would be sleeping on the sofa for a long time."

His parents having sex wasn't something he even wanted to consider. "Telling Mom is one thing. Blabbing to Elana is another. Didn't you think it would be awkward for her—a human—to be told she was destined to be with a bear shifter?"

His father cleared his throat. "She seemed so taken with you that I thought it would be okay."

It wouldn't do any good to rebuke him any further. The harm had already been done, though he had to admit Elana had taken the mating thing a lot better than he'd expected. Then again, he hadn't bitten her yet, so nothing was set in stone. Having his urges grow exponentially as soon as he did bite her wasn't something he could handle right now. "I'll text you tomorrow when we leave the house."

He disconnected then called Izzy, hoping she could provide him with Deanna Landon's number. If he'd had Teagan's number he would have called her instead, as Deanna was her boyfriend Kip's sister.

After a round of phone calls, he received the number he wanted. The big question was whether the psychic would be free tomorrow to go through the Stanley home to recreate the crime scene. When he finally reached her, she seemed more than willing to help.

"Can you meet me at the house tomorrow around ten?" he asked.

"Absolutely."

"Do I need to bring anything with me, like photos?"

"If there are photos in the house from when they were alive, that should suffice."

Worked for him. "See you there tomorrow."

Not wanting to keep Elana waiting, he returned to the living room. She looked up when he walked in. "How did it go?"

"Good. Dad will be your shadow for a while. In the meantime, I'll be meeting Deanna at ten tomorrow morning." Kalan didn't want to dwell on all this negative stuff. It wouldn't be good for her. "You up for a walk around the lake?"

His mind worked better when he was moving, and being surrounded by nature always calmed him. He might even shift and play, though under no circumstances would he let her ride him. He had his pride. When they returned, she could ride him a whole different way.

"I'd love to."

Chapter Seventeen

Kalan stood off to the side watching Deanna do her psychic thing, as she'd asked him not to disturb the air in the room. Apparently, she needed to absorb the energy. She was a tall girl, in her early thirties, with delicate features, and long dark hair. Pretty, but she seemed a bit too serious to enjoy life.

Several photos of the deceased couple were prominently displayed on the mantel, all from their travels, and she studied them for several minutes.

The crime scene unit had cleared the scene, and Kalan didn't tell her where he'd found the bodies or anything about the crime, other than two people had been murdered.

"I'm sensing a lot of anger and pain," she said, "especially around the area of this sofa."

"That was where we found Mrs. Stanley's body."

Deanna faced him. "There are a lot of signatures here too, and it's hard to tell which ones belonged to the homeowners, the killers, and the officers who investigated the crime."

That wasn't good. He didn't see how she would be able to separate all the people then. "If it helps, we believe the murderers were wolf shifters."

"That may help." Deanna walked over to the spot where Richard Stanley had died. "I sense greed right here."

Okay, that was a bit creepy. "Can you tell how many angry people were in the living room at the time of the murder?" That might eliminate the officers.

"I'm sensing five people, two being the victims."

He didn't want to sound excited and throw her off balance, but his heart rate didn't seem to be having any such restraint. "If I show you a picture of one of the men who was here during the murders, can you say if he's the one who actually did the killing?" That was an odd question, but he didn't want say the man claimed his partner had done the actual murder.

"Is it a photograph?"

"It's on my phone."

"I can try."

Kalan retrieved the department's photo of Hank Melton and showed it to her. She placed her hand on the screen, though he didn't know what good that would do.

"I'm getting a weak response, like he wasn't the one responsible for the actual deaths."

Kalan should have taken a picture of the dead man, but it was too late now. He'd spoken with Jackson on the way over and his brother said even the best evidence man wouldn't be able to find where he'd buried the body.

Whoever had murdered Chris Darden had probably come back to dispose of any evidence and ending up killing Darden. While Melton claimed there were only two men present, most likely he was protecting the third person. Possibly someone he feared.

"Can you tell me anything about the other two men?" Chris Darden was of average height, had a round face, and a soft middle, but he'd keep that information to himself for now.

Deanna closed her eyes then squinted them as if the image in her head was blurry. "I see darkness swirling around the one who delivered the final blow, as if he enjoyed the kill. The leader of the three was tall and quite large. Something is wrong with his leg. It might be from a wound or a badly healed bone."

A shifter would have been able to heal himself, though it was possible he was born with a deformity. "That's great." She swayed and grasped the side table. "Are you okay?"

"I'll be fine. This takes a lot of energy, especially when those involved are so dark."

He understood. Even in his human form, he could sense things other humans couldn't. Unfortunately, the number of people who'd been in a room wasn't one of them. "You've been a big help. Thank you."

Once he escorted Deanna out and locked up, he had one more person to talk to before he went into work and began the heaps of paperwork—Brian Stanley. But before he did, Kalan wanted to stop at Elana's store and make sure she was doing okay. He missed her more than he was willing to admit. Having her image pop up randomly made it hard to do his job, and he wondered how Rye had succeeded at first—or had he?

AS MUCH AS Elana enjoyed being back in her store, just knowing that someone had been in her apartment destroying her things had her on edge. She'd spotted Mr. Murdoch a few times across the street and then as he passed by her window. He'd stop, check out the display, and then move on. She'd be the first to admit that his presence provided her with a lot of comfort.

Keeping busy was good for her, but at some point, she'd have to make arrangements for her parents' funeral, and she was still having a difficult time believing they were dead. The silver lining was that providing the flowers for the service wouldn't cost too much. The big question now was if she had a service, would anyone show up? Her parents hadn't been in town long enough to have made any good friends.

The bell above the door chimed and she jerked out of her reverie. When she looked up and found it was Kalan, her pulse soared. His hair was pulled back, and the top was a bit messy as if he'd stabbed his fingers through it many times. She stepped from behind the counter and rushed over to him.

"What are you doing here?"

He laughed. "Is that how you greet your customers?"

If his eyes hadn't twinkled, she would have turned twenty shades of red. "Should I have done this instead?"

As if that witch was standing right behind her, urging her on, Elana wrapped her arms around his neck, drew his head down, and kissed him. His outdoorsy scent had her reeling, and when he pulled her close, she sagged against him. If they weren't in plain view of everyone on the street, she'd have popped open his pants and sucked him dry.

Pulse racing, she opened up and invited him in. Only because his eyes turned amber and his facial hair grew did she step back.

A huge grin split his face. "Now that's a welcome, but only for me, mind you."

She laughed. As if she'd ever be that friendly with anyone else. "We'll see." As she'd hoped, he responded with a growl. "Did you stop by because you missed me?"

"Absolutely, and I thought you'd want to know that I just finished with Deanna."

She'd totally forgotten about the psychic reading. The thought of anyone being at a crime scene as part of her work—or rather at that particular crime scene—had her pulse turning erratic and her chest hurting. "Did she learn anything?"

"She confirmed my suspicions that other than your folks, there were three additional people there the night of your parents' murders."

One was dead and one was in custody. That meant the third man was unaccounted for. From the way his brows rose, that was all the information he was going to provide. "So what's next on your busy cop agenda?"

"I'm on my way to speak with Brian."

At the mention of her brother's name, she sobered. Now would be a good time to tell Kalan her decision. "I want to meet him."

Those raised brows pinched again. "You sure? He said he wasn't planning to stay in town."

"That doesn't surprise me. Did he say anything about wanting to at least meet me?" Kalan looked off to the side, confirming her suspicion. "That's okay. He has no reason to desire a connection with anyone in the Stanley family."

Kalan stroked her cheek, bringing her comfort. "I'll see if he's amenable. It's probably hard for him too. He finally meets his parents after all this time and runs into a murder investigation. His therapist said Brian's been on medication for being bipolar. Add in being anxious and a host of other things, and he might not want to stir the emotional pot anymore."

What Kalan said was right. "I'll respect whatever Brian wants to do. I certainly don't want to make his life any worse."

Kalan cupped her face. "You are a wonderful woman. I'm lucky to have found you."

No one had ever said anything like that to her before, and her heart nearly burst with joy and robbed her of words. *Say something.* "I'm the lucky one. Of all the deputies in Silver Lake, I have you protecting me."

He lifted her chin. "I think the goddess had a hand in that. They knew what I needed—and what I wanted, even if I didn't realize it."

If she'd been made of wax, his sweet words would have melted her into a puddle. "If you learn their heavenly address, I'll send them a thank you note."

He laughed.

The door to Blooms of Hope opened and Izzy rushed in. "Oh! I didn't know were here, Kalan."

There was something about the way Izzy's eyes sparkled that convinced Elana her friend wasn't telling the truth. Izzy had mentioned that once she had learned how to change into her wolf form she could sense when other shifters were near.

Kalan kissed Elana's forehead. "I'll let you two girls chat. I'll see you tonight."

As soon as he disappeared, Izzy's eyes widened. "I think we need to catch up."

Elana had to think back to the last time she'd spoken with her friend. Rye must have told her that he and Kalan had caught the killers. "I don't think we've talked since I met Kalan's family."

"What did you think? Do tell."

Elana detailed how amazing and welcoming they were. "I have to admit, I was shocked when Kalan's father stood, held up his glass in a toast, and then announced I was his son's mate."

"What?" Izzy grabbed her upper arm and gently led her to the back room, presumably where they could have an uninterrupted and secure conversation.

The large table in the middle was splattered with cuttings, baby's breath, and floral foam, but at least the shelves on the opposing walls that contained an assortment of vases, ribbons, stuffed animals, and everything she needed to be creative, were relatively neat.

"He said you were Kalan's mate? That's fantastic." Her face suddenly lost its color. "Does Kalan know?"

"He said he heard the toast, but he hasn't discussed it with me much."

"So he hasn't made it final yet?"

"By biting me?" Izzy nodded. "No."

"He's probably in shock, though he knows you two belong with each other."

Elana moved the shears off to the side and hopped up on the table. "How exactly does a bear shifter know when he's met his mate? What are the signs?"

"Mind you, I learned this after the fact, but the first thing that happens is there is an overwhelming sexual attraction between the two of you—and I don't mean just plain lust."

"I have lust that's quite overwhelming."

Izzy laughed. "It's more than that. The other person almost becomes an obsession." Elana lowered her chin and looked up at Izzy. "Yes, it's similar to what you experienced with Kalan, but this undeniable pull is much worse for *Weres*."

Dear God. "He's always working hard not to shift."

"That's the first sign, and if you mate, it becomes even worse—at least for a while. This might be too much information, but only now are we able to be apart from each other without clawing at the walls when we're at work. But that's taken a couple of weeks."

Kalan was pretty horny all the time too. She wouldn't be able to walk if they had sex more than they already did.

"Well, damn. I guess we are fated mates." She scooted back to get more comfortable. "So tell me what it's like to shift."

THIS MORNING, KALAN had called Brian to say the killers had been caught and to let him know he was free to return to Ohio. Kalan then said he had a few questions for him before Brian took off. While not required by law to answer those questions, Brian agreed to meet with Kalan at twelve thirty in his hotel room.

Kalan hadn't been in the Silver Lake Hotel in a long time, and the corridors seemed darker and narrower than he remembered. The carpet could use a good cleaning too as it smelled a bit musty.

Brian opened the door on the first knock, and he looked even worse than the last time Kalan had spoken with him. His eyes were red and he hadn't shaved. Without saying anything, Brian stepped back to allow Kalan to enter. The beds were made and an open suitcase was on one of them.

"Thanks for seeing me," Kalan said. A two-person table sat in the corner and he dragged out a chair and sat down, trying to put Brian at ease.

"Did you find out who trashed my room? Is that why you're here?" His level of belligerence was sky high, but that was to be expected.

"We have surveillance showing two masked men tearing up the place. While we can't see any distinguishing features, we believe they probably were the same ones who murdered your parents."

"What were they looking for in my room?" Brian remained standing probably because it made him feel more in control.

The case was closed, so Kalan saw no reason not to tell him something. "These two men claim they ordered a rare type of stone from your folks, called red sardonyx. Instead of selling it to them at the agreed price, they had Elana hold it while they tried to haggle for a higher fee."

Brian shook his head. "Assholes. I should be glad they sent me away. If I'd been raised by them, I'd be more fucked up than I already am."

Don't comment.

Kalan was thankful Elana hadn't been emotionally damaged like Brian had been, and his admiration for her grew. "Here's the thing that's been bugging me. How did these men know you might have had the sardonyx they'd purchased?"

"How do I know? I wouldn't recognize the stuff if I saw it, and it's not like my parents gave it to me for safekeeping. Fuck, they wouldn't have given me their trash."

This wasn't getting him anywhere. "I'm thinking you might have met these men, possibly on that first night at your parents. You said they had company." Kalan pulled up the photo of Hank Melton from his phone and held it out. "Was he one of the men who came to your parents' house?"

"Yeah, that was him. He came with two others."

Bingo! There had been three. "Can you describe the other two?"

He glanced to the side. "Not really. I was so frustrated and angry, I didn't really pay attention."

"Did you shake hands with one of them?"

Brian's lip curled. "I guess. Why?"

He wasn't about to explain how that man might have transformed into a Brian look-alike, hoping to point a finger at him as the murderer. "Just wondering. Can you tell me anything about that man?"

Brian stared as his feet and rubbed his fingertips together as if that would retrieve the memory. "He was big and he limped. That's all, other than it didn't look like he'd shaved in a while."

He'd be damned. Deanna Landon had gotten it right.

Chapter Eighteen

ELANA SHIFTED HER weight from side to side. "Brian really said he'd be here?"

Kalan rubbed her shoulder. "When I asked Brian if he was willing to meet you, he said yes. Be patient. He's not late yet."

She bet Kalan had to twist his arm to come. Elana's pits were already damp and she had those stupid butterflies beating inside her. For twenty-seven years, she believed she'd been an only child, and now she was going to come face to face with a man who was her brother.

Kalan stiffened when the front door opened and a man about five-foot nine walked in. With his hands in his pockets, his gaze bounced around, but Elana had no doubt this was Brian. Not only did they have the same blue eyes that were prevalent in the Stanley family, he had the same shaped face as her dad and their mom's long nose.

"Brian?" she said holding out her hand. "I'm Elana."

When he didn't remove his hands from his pockets, she lowered her arm and bit back the disappointment. What had she been thinking? Did she really think he'd throw himself into her arms?

Maybe.

Instead, he just stared at her for a moment and then his shoulders seemed to relax. "I thought you'd look more like Mom. I'm glad you don't."

His comment could have been worse. Her mother had been a

very pretty woman though. Growing up, Elana had always wanted to look like her—at least she had until her teen years. "Want to sit down? I have a booth in back."

His gaze shot to Kalan. "He sitting with us?"

Kalan held up a hand. "No. This is between you two."

The moment Kalan moved away from them, Elana's heart beat faster. A ton of questions bombarded her as she led Brian to her booth in the back of the bar. Anna had been able to mind the store, giving Elana her one shot to connect with Brian before he left town.

Elana slid in and Brian sat across from her. Not knowing what to do with her hands, she placed them on her lap. "Do you want to ask me any questions?"

"Not sure what good it will do now, but yeah. Your cop friend said you had no idea I even existed. Is that true?"

The pain radiating from his voice tore up her insides. "Not that I recall. I'm thinking it was so painful for them to have put you in the mental hospital that they kept quiet about it." She wasn't ready to address the possibility they sent away their first-born child because they were self-centered narcissists. To this day, she questioned why they had her if they knew they weren't going to be spending much time at home. After learning what they had done with Brian, her confusion had increased.

"Bullshit. Those fuckers didn't give a shit about me." He tapped his chest. "Their own son."

Sadly, that might have been true, but Elana pressed her lips together not wanting to make things worse. "When you were with them, did they go on trips and leave you with a different nanny each time?"

He stilled, as if that might be a trick question. "Yes, all the time. My therapist said that was why I acted up. Sure, I had a chemical imbalance in my brain, which is why I have to take pills for being bipolar, but if I'd had loving parents, I wouldn't have been so fucked up."

Her chest hurt for him. She didn't know how to respond, so she reached out to take his hand, but he pulled away, which was as painful as a knife slicing through her heart. "I'm sorry."

"How did you survive?"

In other words, why hadn't she been sent away? "I met a girl in school who had a wonderfully supportive family. They helped me during the tough times. I've always considered them to be my true parents."

Brian leaned back in his seat, his face visibly relaxing. "You were lucky."

"I know."

Brian glanced over at Kalan who was speaking with Finn, Rye's brother. "Is he your man?"

Her man? Brian was probably asking if they were dating. "Yes. After our parents died, the department assigned him to be my bodyguard, and our feelings grew from there."

"Is he treating you okay?"

Whoa. She never expected him to utter those possessive words—words that made her heart flutter. Her parents never asked if a guy she dated treated her well. "Yes. He treats me like a princess."

Elana wanted a drink, but so far none of the servers had come over to take their order. She suspected that Kalan told them to leave the two of them alone.

"What are your plans now?" she asked.

Kalan had told her Brian planned to go back to Ohio, but she hoped he'd want to visit again.

"I'll be returning home tomorrow. I have a job there."

How sad that she knew so little about him. "What do you do for a living?"

"I work at a lumberyard."

"Sounds nice." Assuming one loved the outdoors. Hopefully, he worked inside in the winter.

They spent the next half hour talking about some of his childhood memories, most of which weren't good. He did have one friend, Danny Reverlo, who made life bearable for a while, but he'd moved away when Brian was six.

Her brother slapped his palms on the table indicating their time together was over. "I'm happy for you," he said, sliding out of his seat. "You survived."

That she had. "Do you think you'll be back?"

"To Silver Lake? There's nothing here for me."

His words hurt, but she totally understood why he'd think that since he'd only known her but a few minutes. "You have me."

"Sure." That one word sounded hollow.

Before Elana could stand and hug him goodbye, he turned and strode out of the bar. Tears burned her eyes, but she refused to cry. Meeting her brother had been a wonderful gift, and she needed to appreciate it for what it was. Would she have liked an emotional reunion with a promise they'd keep in touch? Sure. But Brian was too damaged.

As soon as her brother left, Kalan strode over, helped her up, and then hugged her. "I think you made a difference."

He couldn't know it, but his comment soothed the ache. Elana held on for dear life, hugging him back. Not wanting to make a scene, she looked up at him. "I hope so."

"You hungry?"

"Starving." It was close to six and she'd skipped lunch.

"If you don't mind, I'd rather not eat here as it's a bit noisy. How about we go to the Lake Steakhouse?"

That was the most expensive restaurant in town. Normally, she would have suggested something cheaper, but her nerves were on edge, and a good meal with a quiet atmosphere would do wonders to calm her down. "I'd love that."

They hopped in his Jeep and headed south on Rivers Edge. A quick jog onto Oak took them to High Point Street where they parked. As they walked down the sidewalk to the restaurant, she reflected on today. To say it had been a rollercoaster of emotions would have been an understatement. Having Kalan stop by around noon had started her day off well—really well. The passionate kiss alone would have made a great diary entry.

Then Izzy had stopped by. Not only had they discussed questions Elana had about this whole shifter-mating thing, her friend had offered to handle the details of her parents' funeral. That alone lightened her burden. After a lengthy discussion, they both decided to have a small service with just her and the Bertas.

For the rest of the afternoon, her shop had been swamped with customers, which kept her mind off of her problems and brought in the much-needed sales. However, what she really needed was some down time to absorb everything that had happened.

Kalan opened the heavy wooden door to the restaurant, and the rich scent of beef and something sweet made her mouth water. The lights were low and most of the dark wooden booths sat vacant. Each table was covered with a white linen cloth, on top of which was a lit candle. It was very romantic. A large ethanol fireplace took up the middle of the room with booths surrounding it. To the left was the bar where she, Missy, and Teagan used to come for happy hour every week or two. Several glassed-in private rooms resided along the back wall, and on the east side was the open grill.

As the hostess ushered them to a booth across from the fireplace, Kalan placed a hand on her back, reminding her once more how lucky she was to have him walk into her life. He then waited until she was seated before slipping in across from her.

"What was it like to meet your brother?"

"I don't think it has sunk in yet. I mean, I've always wanted a brother or a sister, but Brian is still a stranger."

Kalan unraveled the silverware from the napkin and placed it on his lap. "Family isn't always the one who has given birth to you."

"I couldn't agree more." Izzy, Missy, and Mr. and Mrs. Berta were her true family.

"I know this might be too soon, but have you given any thought to what you're going to do with the house?"

Another weight dropped onto her shoulders. "I plan to sell it, as I never want to live there ever again." She visibly shook.

"Smart. I'm sure there are too many bad memories associated with that place."

"Definitely." Their server stopped by, and Kalan ordered a beer while she asked for a Merlot. Elana didn't want to discuss problems associated with the home. It was too depressing. "So tell me. Do you eat a lot of fish?" He was a bear after all. It shouldn't really matter, but the more she understood about the bear culture, the better she'd feel.

It took a few seconds for him to understand why she was asking before he cracked up laughing. "Because of my other persona?" He whispered the last word.

"Yes. It's a reasonable question."

"For your information, I like fish, chicken, beef, and everything else just like any normal man."

Sometimes, Kalan seemed more bear than man to her. "Besides that cute transformative trick you do, are you able to do anything similar to what Izzy can?" Izzy had trained her to use code words to describe the Wendayan talents. Elana would have to be just as careful in public if she had to discuss anything related to werebears.

"I'm afraid not. Izzy transferred some of her talents to Rye, which means he can do some really cool things the rest of us can't."

If Kalan ever decided to mate with her, he'd get nothing in return, which wasn't really fair to him. Perhaps that was why he hadn't bitten her.

Don't dwell on that. I need to be thankful he's with me now.

Once their drinks arrived, Kalan held up his glass. "May your life be smooth sailing from here on out."

"Wouldn't that be nice." She sipped her wine then set it down. "I don't think I told you that the men working on my apartment said they'd be finished in a few days."

"That's great." His voice sounded cheerful, but his eyes had darkened.

In the short time she'd come to know him, it seemed that his eyes changed color depending on his mood. Super excited, and they were amber; angry, and his eyes turned a forest green. Right now they bordered on the dark side.

If he didn't want her to move back to her apartment, he should say something. Stupid man.

Their server came for their dinner order. She ordered a steak, and Kalan picked out the salmon. She swore he did it just to mess with her mind. Elana was bursting with so many more questions about what it was like to be a shifter, how old he was when he first shifted, and did it hurt when he changed shape—but a restaurant wasn't the place to discuss those kinds of things. Besides, Kalan seemed a little distracted, so she sipped her wine and waited for their meal to arrive.

"I'd like you to move in with me," Kalan said out of the blue.

"Excuse me?"

"I know the danger is mostly over, but I'd feel better if you stayed with me. You're too alone above your shop."

As she studied the color of his eyes, his lips twitched on one side. What did that mean? His motive for asking remained a mystery. Was it merely his protective instinct that made him ask, or did he really want to give the two of them a chance to learn about each other and fall in love?

"Why?"

"It's obvious isn't it?"

Because I'm your mate? "Not to me."

He leaned forward, planted his elbows on the table, and then glanced around, probably to make sure no one was listening. "I can't think straight when I'm away from you. You dominant my every thought."

It took a moment to unravel the double negative. "Because you're worried about me?"

"Yes, I'm worried about you, but it's more than that. You are like my compass, helping me focus on what's important."

He dragged a hand down his head, probably to smooth the wisps of hair that had escaped the band. Failing to tame his beautiful locks, he ripped off the tie and his hair fell about his shoulders. She could watch him do that move a hundred times a day and not grow tired of it.

"What exactly is important to you?" She didn't want to sound dense, but she needed to hear the words.

"You are. I want to be with you. It's not just about the sex either," he whispered. "It's how I feel when I'm with you. I'm more alive than I've ever been before."

That worked for her. "Then I say yes!"

Chapter Nineteen

AFTER THEIR HUGE meal at the Lake Steakhouse, Kalan insisted they stop at the grocery store for some brownie mix. The whole idea of baking something together really appealed to her, but it would mean Elana would have to do something later about cutting back on all those extra calories.

With a bag full of ingredients in hand, he opened his front door and motioned she go in first.

"Your dad told me you didn't know how to cook."

His eyes widened. "Are you kidding me? Didn't I make the best hot dogs on this side of the lake?"

She laughed. "You did. Perhaps you should cook something for him and show him."

He tapped her nose then set the bag on the counter. "I just might."

"What can I do to help?"

"First, I need to read the instructions on the box." He removed it from the bag and as he read the ingredients out loud, she organized them on the counter then turned on the stove.

Together, they located the bowl and mixer. It didn't take long to make the batter and then grease the dish. Before she had the chance to put the bake pan in the heated oven, Kalan stuck his finger in the batter and licked it. "Yum."

As long as he had a taste, she wanted one too. She scooped up two fingers full of the mix, but before she even opened her mouth,

Kalan leaned over and sucked it off her fingers. Instant heat soared through her at that action, flooding her system with hormones.

"That's not fair. That was my taste."

He grinned. "I'll give you your taste."

He stepped back, unzipped his trousers, and then stepped out of them. Elana was speechless at the huge bulge in his briefs. The man seemed to be in a perpetual state of arousal. Izzy's words came back to her about the effect a mate had on her man. Holy shit. To think they weren't even mated yet. Heaven help her if he ever bit her.

Hooking his fingers in his briefs, he kept his gaze on her face as he eased them down—inch by excruciatingly slow inch.

"Need help?" She licked her lips, hoping he'd get the hint.

"In a moment. The animal in me wants you too fucking much right now."

She planted her hands on her hips. "I want the *man* in you to want me."

"Oh, baby, he wants you more."

Kalan knew how to sweet-talk her. Once he'd discarded his briefs, he reached over to the brownie mix and swiped a large glob then slathered it on his cock.

"That's what I'm talking about," she said.

"Fair's fair. Since I stole your lick, how about tasting this?"

Uh-oh. His eyes turned a golden hue and his eyeteeth poked out of his mouth, but she had to trust his bear wouldn't escape.

As if she were bobbing for apples, Elana clasped her hands behind her back and leaned over. The scent of chocolate had her salivating. Not wanting the batter to drip, she began her adventure at the base of his cock and licked upward.

"Fuck, that feels so good." He grabbed her shoulder and groaned.

This was fun and tasty. She decided the only way to get all of it was to devour his cock, but that would require her hands. Unclasping her fingers, she pulled his big shaft closer and then sucked on him hard, swirling her tongue around and around to get every bit of chocolate.

"Enough." Kalan lifted her by the shoulders. "I can't wait any longer."

As he undid the buttons on her shirt, his gaze never left her face. If she hadn't wanted to impress Brian, she would have donned a T-shirt—one that was easy to remove. With each button Kalan unhooked, he moved her backward until she bumped into the counter.

"Never doubt my desire for you. You are what I need. What I want."

He'd said that before, but Elana hadn't wanted to believe it could possibly be true, because she didn't want to be disappointed if he lost interest later on. Though at the moment, that didn't seem likely. "Okay."

She wished she could come up with a better response, but right now his cock was pressed against her belly disrupting her ability to think, much less express herself.

Kalan finished unbuttoning her blouse, slid it off her shoulders, and then tossed it aside. Hopefully, it didn't land in the brownie mix. She might have looked had he not leaned over and kissed her. The moment their lips touched, she pressed her chest against his, and heat spread like wildfire.

He reached around her back and unhooked her bra. The thought of his roving tongue across her breast and then sucking on her nipples had her damp with need. With her clean hand, she grabbed a fistful of his thick, wavy hair, and its silkiness turned her on.

Kalan lowered the straps on her bra then leaned back. "You make me wild."

"Ditto."

As much as she wanted to touch him, she didn't want to break the incredible connection they were experiencing. He slipped off her bra and let it fall to the floor. "I need you higher."

After shoving the mixing bowl and the empty brownie box out of the way, he lifted her onto the counter. He then leaned over, and when he sucked on one breast, tiny explosions of need shot in every direction.

He stopped his delicious assault. "Wait. I have a better idea."

What could be better than what he'd been doing? Kalan stepped over to the batter—which she now suspected would never be made—scooped some with his forefinger then dragged it across her other nipple.

He blew out a long breath. "All mine."

Lowering his head again, he sucked, twirled, and devoured the batter off her hardened tip. Just listening to his moans and grunts, her need ratcheted. At the pressure he was exerting on her body, she was forced to lean back on her elbows. With this new angle, she could wrap her legs around his waist. Too bad, she was still clothed.

Seconds later, he must have recognized the dilemma for he undid the button on her jeans, unzipped them, and then tugged them off. "Zebra striped. Nice. Maybe I can find you ones with bear paw prints on them."

How cute would that be? "I'd gladly wear them."

"Right now, I need you wearing nothing." In a flash, her panties disappeared.

He lifted her legs onto his shoulder, forcing her onto her back. He grabbed her blouse from the counter, rolled it into a ball, and placed it under her head. That was definitely more comfortable. "Thank you."

"Let me show you my appreciation." His eyes lightened and his hair fell into his face as he leaned forward and swiped a tongue across her opening.

Bursts of pleasure ran rampant inside her, and she had to grip the edge of the countertop to keep some control as each lick and flick brought her closer to her climax. What was wrong with her? She'd never been this sensitive in her life. With Kalan things were so different…more wonderful, special, amazing.

"Take me," she gasped.

"Easy."

"I am not easy. Okay, I am with you, but if you want me, you have to make love with me now."

He sucked on her clit once more, heating her to the max. "Only because I don't want you to suffer will I honor your request."

"You're full of shit. You can't last either. Your facial hair is thicker and those teeth look mighty sharp." Damn. She never should have tossed out that dare. Now, he might withhold the prize.

Kalan responded by lowering her legs and wrapping them around his waist again. "Let's test that theory of yours. Hold on."

Score! Reaching under her, he lifted her off the counter. She grabbed onto his broad shoulders for support and planted her feet on his thighs. By sitting up straighter, she was able to reach his delicious lips. His arms tightened around her, and he kissed her hard and with so much passion that it released every feminine hormone in her body. As their tongues dueled and each fought for position, joy burst from within.

He then reached below them and adjusted the tip of his cock so that it was at her entrance. The anticipation made her even wetter.

When he didn't try to impale her, she widened her legs a bit and dropped down on him, immediately closing her eyes to keep from hyperventilating. She swore he was bigger than ever before.

As soon as the pulsing and throbbing subsided, Kalan eased out and drove into her again, sending a cascade of pure bliss through her. He lowered his head and loosened his grip, allowing her to lean back. The first tug on her nipple had her soaring. God, it was hard enough to keep from coming with his big cock inside her let alone after he added the glorious nipping and teasing on her tits.

He growled and plowed into her again. While his scruff looked closer to a beard, she wanted him even more desperate, so she clamped down hard on his cock.

His mouth opened, and he sucked in an audible breath. "That's it. I can't…control… it any more."

His hands slid to her waist, and she increased the pressure on the sides of his legs to keep from slipping. Together, they rode each other hard, until her oxygen-starved brain yelled his name when her orgasm rushed in. Kalan drew her close and kissed her again just as he released his hot seed. She closed her eyes, and as the light show begin, her whole body felt as if she'd been transported to another dimension—one in which she could romp free.

He drew her closer and kissed her temple, her forehead, and then he finally lightly brushed her lips with his. "I can't stay away from you."

"Is that a problem?"

He chuckled. "It is if you ever want to be able to leave the house again." He withdrew and slid her back onto the counter.

She let her imagination run wild. Tangled sheets, morning coffee, and then more sex. She saw nothing wrong with that.

Grabbing a dry towel from a drawer, he wet it and cleaned them up. She nodded to the dish full of brownie mix. "What do you say we bake what's left? I've built up a big appetite after that."

"A woman after my own heart."

ELANA WAS IN a deep sleep, dreaming of running in the woods with Kalan, when someone shook her shoulder. She moaned then opened her eyes to find a neatly groomed Kalan in his uniform, and her energy immediately perked up. "Hi."

Even though her shop was open, she took off Mondays, which meant she could sleep in.

He leaned over and kissed her. "I debated letting you sleep, but I have to go into work for a bit. I shouldn't be long. Will you be okay by yourself?"

"Sure." Izzy had to work, so there'd be no sharing of stories, but she could read. "Do you have a problem if I wander to the lake?"

"It's safe all around here." He smiled then walked out of the room.

Damn. Even though their lovemaking had been epic last night, she wouldn't have minded a few more caresses this morning. She checked the clock on the nightstand and was dismayed to find it was almost eleven. Yikes.

She jumped out of bed, quickly showered, and then dressed in something summery. Kalan said he wouldn't take long, so perhaps they could go for a walk after he returned. Wanting to look sexy for him, she picked something low cut to show off her breasts, since he really seemed to relish them. The empire top hid a lot of her flaws, as did the cute capris pants.

Hungry, she headed into the kitchen and spotted the plate of brownies. Needing the jolt of sugar, she practically inhaled one while she made coffee then poured a bowl of cereal.

Needing to pass the time, she pulled out her phone and found a love story she'd read many times before. Getting lost in another world through reading fiction had been the main thing that had kept her sane during her youth.

Once she ate and cleaned up, she found a comfy spot on the sofa and read. It was well past one when the doorbell rang and she smiled. Kalan must have forgotten his house key. He said he never locked the door before she'd moved in and probably wasn't in the habit of carrying it with him.

"Coming."

She set aside her phone, ran her hands down her hair to smooth it and then pulled open the door. Her breath caught. It wasn't Kalan, and her pulse shot up. "May I help you?"

The man had a pad of paper in his hand, along with a pen. Wearing a blue suit of worsted wool, he appeared overly dressed for summer. "I'm collecting for the animal shelter in town. We've had an increase in abused dogs brought in lately that need treatment, and I was wondering if you could spare a donation of even five dollars?"

Elana watched every dime she had, but the animal shelter was one charity she could never resist. However, something about the man set off warning signals. "I already donated. Thank you." She eased closed the door but was immediately met with resistance.

Thinking she'd bumped into something, she pulled the door

back to check, when the man on the other side shoved it open. His calm countenance was gone, replaced by a scowl.

"I know you have the stone. I want it."

Holy shit, holy shit, holy shit! This must be the third man who murdered her parents. "I don't have it."

The hard slap across her face sent her reeling and her pulse soaring. In an attempt to move away from him, she tripped on the area rug and went tumbling onto her butt. The hard landing jarred her, causing pain shoot up her spine. Her chest constricted, and she couldn't get air. Her mind said to speak to him in a reasonable manner, but the adrenaline rush in her body insisted she flee.

Before she could decide what to do, he lifted her up by the arm. "I asked you a question. Where is the sardonyx?"

Chapter Twenty

KALAN WAS ON his way back to Elana when his cell rang. His future mate probably wanted to know when he would be coming home. He hadn't meant to take so long at the station, but the paperwork involved with switching out Hank Melton's high security ankle monitor took longer than he'd expected.

Rye had called this morning to say he'd secured a special ankle monitor for the Changeling that would inhibit his ability to touch someone and transform into his clone during the red moon. Kalan wasn't about to ask where or how Rye had found one that could be altered, but apparently, he'd called in a few Alpha favors.

Apparently, Izzy had contacted Ophelia who said she could line the bracelet with rose quartz by transforming it into a malleable substance just long enough for her to place it in the ankle monitor. When the stone came in contact with the Changeling's body, his powers would be diminished significantly. Ophelia said it was possible that Hank Melton might not even be able to shift at all.

If all Changelings could be captured and monitored in such a way, the world would be a better place.

Another shrill tone of the phone jarred him back to the present. Kalan lifted his cell from his pocket, about to make some sexy remark, when he noticed the caller ID read Private Caller.

"Detective Murdoch."

"Kalan, it's Teagan."

Her shaky voice had him gripping the wheel tighter, and every one of his senses sharpened. "What is it?"

"This may be nothing, but I had another vision about Elana."

This couldn't be good. None of her visions had been. "What did you see?"

Elana had mentioned that Teagan's last vision involved Elana turning into some kind of stone statue in a field, and that something big and fast would rush in and save her. Fortunately, that crazy image had never materialized.

"I saw Elana's face, and then suddenly, darkness surrounded her. It was really evil. My vision was strong—really strong—which means it might be happening now."

Blood pounded in his ears. "I'm on my way to her." He disconnected before she had the chance to say more.

Fuck. He hadn't wanted to leave Elana this morning, and if Rye hadn't called with something so important, he would have stayed home with her.

Being a cop, Kalan tried to obey all the traffic rules, but when the light heading toward his house turned yellow, Kalan sped up. Horns honked. Too bad. This was an emergency. If he'd been in the cruiser instead of his Jeep, they would have understood.

Imagining the worst, his pulse soared. Once through the entrance to his compound, he took the next turn too fast, and two of the wheels lifted off the pavement, but he managed to right the vehicle. When he pulled into his driveway, he slammed on his brakes. The front door stood wide open and he nearly shifted from fear. He jumped out and took off.

The wolf signature nearby made him hurry, but it was Elana's scream coming from out back that had him changing direction. If Rye had been here, he'd have shifted immediately into his wolf form, as he was faster that way. As a lumbering bear, Kalan possessed strength but not a whole lot of speed.

The moment he rounded the corner at the back of his house, he spotted Elana rushing across the back of the property, arms flaying, running for her life. A sharp spike pierced his heart. Right behind her, a man was coming out of the house through the sliding glass door.

They made eye contact, and instantly the intruder shifted into his wolf form, and Kalan followed suit by changing into his bear. Adrenaline pouring through his veins, along with just the right amount of anger, Kalan charged across the yard.

The wolf leaped onto the porch railing and shoved off. Before he even landed on the ground, Kalan reached him and swiped a claw across the wolf's jaw. The animal yelped. He then bounced back onto his paws and charged. After years of sparring with Rye, Kalan was aware of just about every move a wolf could make. Given that Rye was highly trained and this wolf was not, this fight should be short lived. Besides, the quartz in the lake would make this wolf less effective as a fighter.

Just as Kalan was ready to take the fatal blow, the animal took off after Elana. Halfway to the forest, she stopped and bent over, her back heaving.

He wanted to shout at her to look up, but all he could do was roar. She must have understood, for she looked up, spun around and continued toward the forest. Kalan darted after the wolf who was now losing speed. The pink quartz must have taken hold because the wolf shifted into his human form. He stumbled and landed on his knees as if all of his energy had drained.

Kalan didn't stop. He barreled toward the man, needing to save Elana, his mate—or at least she would be just as soon as he sunk his teeth into her tender little neck.

His protective nature spurred him on. The man sprinted toward Elana, and somehow managed to shift into his wolf once more. She reached the dense forest, but when she came to the old Oak tree, she halted. Hooking a foot into the crook, she leveraged herself upward. While the wolf might jump up at her, she should be high enough to be safe—unless the wolf shifted once more.

The animal slowed and circled the tree, probably deciding his next move. Those few seconds enabled Kalan to take one big leap with his claws extended and land on the wolf's back. Trapped, the wolf cried. As much as Kalan wanted to torture the man's human half and demand answers, he'd not take the chance the intruder escaped.

When the wolf stilled, Kalan retracted his claws so he could roll him over, exposing his throat. The only way to kill one of these fuckers was to rip it out. As much as he didn't want Elana to see the violent side of him, he had no choice.

In one bite, the deed was done.

He stepped back and watched to make sure the animal bled out. After the wolf's last breath, he returned to his human form. Kalan then shifted and spit out the blood.

Goddess, with his mouth all bloody, he must look a frightful mess. Kalan moved closer to the tree. He swiped an arm across his mouth, but all that did was smear it more. "Elana, it's okay. Come on down, baby. He can't hurt you anymore."

He reached up, but she held on tight. "I'm afraid to let go."

"You don't need to be. Jump and I'll catch you. I promise."

Kalan didn't think she would, but a second later she was in his grasp with her arms wrapped tightly around him. "I was so scared. That horrid man wanted the sardonyx. I probably would have given it to him if I had known the combination to the safe."

"Shh. You did great." Since two people had been murdered, and now two more were dead and one incarcerated, that piece of stone sure was valuable. "Maybe we should put it in a museum and let them keep it secure."

A small smile lifted her lips. "Perhaps." She lifted her head. "Oh, you're naked, by the way."

"Yeah, well that happens when I shift."

She sniffed. "I like that fact about you, but I could do without the blood."

"I'll wash up." He was pleased Elana seemed to have somewhat recovered. She was an amazing woman, one he wanted by his side—forever. Her whole life had been a series of roadblocks, yet she'd persevered. He could only hope he could now bring her the joy she deserved.

Once back inside, he finally set her down and headed straight for the kitchen sink. He splashed water on his face, rinsed his mouth, and washed his hands. He snagged a clean towel from the drawer and wiped as much of the blood off him as possible then dumped it in the trash. "I'm sorry I got blood on you. We both need to wash. Want to join me in the shower?"

She slipped an arm through his. "Is there room?"

"Most of the houses in this area were built with a large master shower with two shower heads."

"That sounds so decadent."

"It is when I get to share it with my beautiful woman. But I need a sec to make a call. While that man out there deserves to have his flesh eaten by an animal, I should take care of his body."

Her brows pinched. "You can't take him to the morgue?"

"I could, but I'd need to make sure Jefferson Williams is there. He's a shifter and won't ask how the man's throat was ripped out by a bear. The bigger issue is that because he died on my land, I'd have to fill out a series of reports to explain how the man was there in the first place."

Elana sagged against him. "He's not worth it."

"That's what I love about you. You understand our culture so well."

"Is that the only thing you love about me?" Her eyes sparkled with mischief.

He laughed. She was so wonderful. If any other woman had asked him that question, he'd have balked and taken off running, but not anymore. He wanted Elana to know what she meant to him. "Far from it. You are ambitious, determined, and sexy as hell. You're adaptable, feisty, spontaneous, and charming." Her face turned a pretty shade of pink.

"Enough. Are you just saying those things because you think I'm fragile right now and need to hear those wonderful words?"

"If you have to ask then you don't know me all that well. I don't bullshit. I love you, Elana Stanley, and in a few minutes, I'm going to show you just how much."

His pulse turned erratic waiting for her response. From the shine in her eyes, she understood exactly what was about to happen. If she didn't want to be bitten, this was her chance to back down.

"I'm ready. But don't you have to make that call first?"

"Shit. I should, but that piece of crap can stay out there a little bit longer. I need to shower and then satisfy my woman." His bear was clamoring for Kalan to claim his mate, but getting clean had to come first.

Not wanting to chance she'd believe Kalan Murdoch, the man, didn't want her, he had to take it slow.

He carried her into the bathroom then set her down. It wasn't grand by any measure, but it was more spacious than the guest bath.

Elana scoped out the place, fingering the towels and running her fingers along the tiled walls. "This is really nice."

"I retiled the bathroom a few years ago and changed out the fixtures." He turned on both showerheads to let the water warm then brushed his teeth. The shower would take care of the other evidence of the fight.

"What if someone finds the body in the meantime?" she asked. "You could be exposed."

Clearly, this was upsetting her, and it tore at him. "Only shifters live around the lake."

"I didn't know that."

"If it will put you at ease, I'll contact Rye now and ask him to put the body somewhere safe." His Alpha owed him.

She smiled. "Thank you. Seeing that dead body gave me the willies."

Poor thing. If he could have finished off the wolf any other way, he would have. With the wolf's dried blood on him, he stepped into the shower and soaped up while she undressed. As if Elana was trying to come to grips with what happened, she seemed to be taking her time neatly folding her clothes then placing them on the counter.

Kalan briefly telepathed Rye what happened and asked if he could remove the body from the property.

"I'm on it," Rye answered back.

"Thanks."

Kalan tapped the glass and motioned her in.

"You said you'd contact Rye," she said as she stepped in next to him.

Mate.

Kalan had to concentrate to ignore his bear. In a few minutes, he'd be shutting up the animal inside him just as soon as Elana became his—forever.

"I just did—with my mind." He grabbed another handful of soap and scrubbed his body once more, determined to rid his skin of that nasty Changeling's blood.

Her chin dipped. "Izzy said she and Rye could communicate with their minds because they were mates, but that no one other than mates could." She dipped her head under the water and wet her hair. She looked so beautiful all wet and slick.

His dick throbbed and he nearly roared. Kalan needed to send a thank you to Izzy for easing Elana into the shifter world. "That's all true, with one exception. An Alpha and his Beta are able to communicate by telepathy. It only started happening between us after our parents announced they were stepping down."

"That is really cool."

He'd never mentioned his position in the Clan. "Did Izzy tell you that I was the Clan's Beta?"

She glanced off to the side. "I kind of wormed it out of her."

He wondered what else his wonderful woman knew. Maybe after their shower, he'd have to exact more information out of her. He was looking forward to that fun.

Chapter Twenty-One

ELANA'S HEAD WAS still spinning. Kalan Murdoch was in love with her? She probably should have asked when he decided that because there were still times when she couldn't figure him out. If what he said was true—that they were to become mates—then she'd have plenty of time to learn everything about him.

His mother had said the process wasn't painful, and hopefully she was right.

"Do you usually turn on both showers when you're in here?"

"No. In fact, I never have because I've never had someone else in my shower before. I had it built in the hopes I could share it with my mate someday." His gaze was as intense as a laser as he scanned her body from head to toe and smiled.

Feeling brazen, she tapped her chest, needing to hear the words. "You mean me?"

"Yes, I mean you, though technically that particular aspect has not occurred yet. Are you okay with that? It'll mean you'll be stuck with me for life."

She clapped then immediately sobered. "What if you grow tired of me?"

Kalan dragged her near, the water beating against her shoulder. "That ain't going to happen, babe. Now get clean, so we can move to a more comfortable location and begin."

In between the two showers was an indented shelf with liquid soap, shampoo, and conditioner, all of which were expensive brands.

It was no wonder Kalan had such nice hair.

She poured a palm full of shampoo on her head. Out of the corner of her eye, she caught Kalan staring at her. His cock was erect and his chest had sprouted more hair.

"Kalan, be good. You said you wanted us to shower first."

"I do, but I can't help but watch you. You are so beautiful."

His words almost seemed painful for him to say, like he was trying not to become excited. Looking at the outward signs, he was failing miserably. She was in the same state of arousal too. The water running down his glorious body made her use all of her control just to finish.

Elana turned her back to the water and finished lathering her hair. The moment she closed her eyes, Kalan's hands brushed hers away. "Let me."

No man had ever washed her hair before, but if it had to be someone, she'd choose Kalan. His fingers gently massaged her scalp, and then he lifted her hair to let the water rinse it clean. His close proximity had her imagination running wild. She pictured him sucking on her nipples, licking her clit, and then impaling her. At the peak of their passion, he'd bite her and Kalan would finally be hers.

When her hair was thoroughly rinsed, she faced him. "How about I wash yours?"

"Already did it, but I can think of some other body parts that need to be cleaned."

She wagged a finger, loving his playful side. "I see what you're trying to do."

"What am I trying to do?" His innocent look came off as comical.

"You want me to touch your cock."

He laughed, poured the body wash onto his hand then rubbed the liquid on her breasts. "You want to and you know it."

She did, but she was determined not to touch him until they were in the bedroom. However, each swirl with his palm on her sensitive skin made her want to shut off the water and do him right there.

Her internal sass meter shot up. "It all depends on whether you can turn me on. I heard *Weres* lacked control around their potential mates, but since humans don't have those kinds of urges, you'll have to be creative."

Elana was rather proud of the way she was able to keep a straight face.

"What a shame you lack a sex drive. That's all the more reason why I need to claim you. Once I sink my teeth into that pretty neck of yours, you won't be able to go an hour without ripping off my clothes and demanding satisfaction."

Dear God, she hoped it wouldn't be that bad. "Really?"

He slipped a hand between her thighs and slid a finger into her needy sex. As much as she wanted to withhold the groan and pretend nothing he did could affect her, a moan slipped out.

"Ah ha! Wait until I drive my cock deep inside you. Before you know it, you'll be clawing at me, begging me to take you every time we're together."

"I thought this mating thing was a two-way street. Are you sure your sex drive won't be affected?"

His body sagged, and he removed his finger. Drawing up to his full height, he reached behind her and turned off her shower, while leaving his running. "I hope you know I'm just kidding with you? I've been told that my sex drive will ramp up to unimaginable levels, but please know that even if my bear is pushing to mate with you, my human side desperately wants and needs you too. I love you so much. I want you, Elana, now and forever."

That was just what Elana needed to hear. She threw her arms around his neck and kissed him hard. He had made her the happiest woman in the world. Their tongues touched, but this time their dance was slow and loving, as if they each wanted to savor every scent and taste. Only because she was bursting to tell him did she break the kiss.

"I love you too, Kalan, and I'm not saying that because you said it first. I think I fell in love with you before we even spoke in the hospital."

"Really?"

He actually sounded surprised. She reached around and shut off his water. "If you let me dry you off, I'll show you how much."

"No man could say no to that offer." He slid back the glass door and motioned she step out first.

Elana grabbed a blue towel from the rack. "It's warm."

"Yup. I like only the best," he said with his gaze on her face, acting as if he was talking about her instead of the towel.

As she rubbed her breasts, Kalan's body began to transform. He turned his back to her. "Want to dry this side first?" he asked.

She laughed. "You're not acting, are you?"

"About wanting you so bad that I'll shift?"

"Uh-huh."

"No."

Joy spread from her toes right up to her heart. "I'll try not to entice you then."

She dragged the thick terrycloth down his back then dropped to one knee to reach his muscular calves and ankles. Once she finished the right side, she moved to the left, drying him from the bottom up. Once she patted his shoulders dry, she turned him around, but he had his eyes closed.

"Why aren't you looking?" she asked.

"If I see you, I'll want you too much," he said.

Elana was taken aback by his sincerity. "Then don't watch. Just feel."

Deciding to let the rest of him air dry, she leaned over and licked his cock. In two seconds flat, she was in the air and then onto his shoulder in a fireman's hold. "That will not dry me. You are in serious trouble now."

While the trip into his bedroom wasn't exactly comfortable, she was laughing too hard to ask him to put her down. Without warning, she was airborne again, and then her back met the bed.

Kalan slid next to her then pulled her on top. "My need is so great that if I do what I want right now, I might hurt you. I need you to take control this time."

The whole idea that she could do what she wanted to Kalan excited her beyond belief. "You'll regret that concession."

He growled, showing her his teeth that had started to sharpen.

Don't think about the bite.

He'd stopped her before when she'd licked him, but maybe now he'd let her do more. She sat up and then slid down, placing her knees between his legs. With his gaze lasered on her, she grabbed his stiff cock and drew it close.

"Don't stay down there too long if you want me inside you."

That was a bluff. He'd never gone off before she was ready. "I'll be careful."

Excitement sizzling inside her, she bent down and drew him into her mouth. Kalan groaned and grabbed a handful of her hair, his breath quickening and his abs tightening, as if he really were fighting for control.

Not wanting this mating process to go wrong, she lifted up and proceeded to lick her way up his abs, taking a second to enjoy the water that had pooled in his belly button. She glanced up at him. His lips were pressed tightly together, and his eyes seemed to be glowing more intensely than usual.

Just as she was about to swipe a tongue across his hardened nipple, he clasped her shoulders and dragged her upward. Chest to chest, he kissed her, seeming to need the contact to keep him centered.

His lips barely touching hers, he ran his hands down her back and whispered, "I love how you smell and how soft your skin is."

"I love everything about you."

His eyes opened wider. "Show me. Ride me hard, baby."

He didn't have to ask her twice. Scooting onto her knees, she lifted up and placed his cock at her damp entrance. Suddenly, the air seemed heavier, and she had a hard time even remembering to breathe. This was it. The moment she'd been dreaming of for years—the day she caught her bear.

Opening wide, she slid down on his huge shaft, stretching her so much, her stomach contracted.

"Easy, baby," Kalan said as he rubbed her arms.

While she loved him being inside her, what she really needed was for him to deflate a bit. He must have sensed her discomfort, for he drew her closer, and the change in angle brought relief. When he lifted his head and drew her nipple into his mouth, her inner walls seemed to expand on their own, accommodating his wide girth.

His hands slid to her hips and held her still while he eased out slowly. The strain around his eyes convinced her he was working hard not to shift, and she decided not to test his resolve anymore.

She leaned forward and kissed him. The second their tongues touched and their scents blended, it was as if the two of them had melded into one being. He lifted up as she slid down. His groan and the tightening of his fingers made her relent and allow him to guide the speed—or at least that had been her plan until he broke the kiss and nibbled his way down her chin and across her jawline.

If she hadn't needed her hands for balance, she would have threaded her fingers through his hair. After he finished exploring, all she could do was lower her head to his neck and inhale his animal scent. Everything about this man was making her lose all control.

His teeth pressed against the soft spot between her shoulder and her neck, and before she could tense up, he drove his cock into her again, igniting every inch of her body. The pressure from his teeth increased, but right now, her climax was building to a point where she wasn't sure she could keep from coming. Her moans and groans matched his grunts and growls.

The second his teeth sunk into her neck, her vision turned black and her oxygen starved brain seemed to enter a new realm where colors were sharper, smells more intense, and her hormones surged so hard, her orgasm burst inside her.

His cock jettisoned its hot cum, forcing her to gulp in much needed air. So feral was her response, she believed that if she hadn't been looking at her human hands, she would have thought she had turned into an animal.

Her body gave way and she collapsed on his chest, her breath heaving. His heartbeat was rapid too, as his arms tightened around her.

"You are my mate, forever."

Glory be.

Chapter Twenty-Two

ELANA COULDN'T BELIEVE how six weeks could change a person so much. Yes, she was sad for what had happened to her parents, but she and her folks had been so disconnected that the love had never formed as it should have. Her whole life, she had always tried to please them, but with their deaths, that part of her was gone. No longer needing to change for anyone, Elana now had a happy life with great friends. The best part was that her love for Kalan knew no bounds.

Perhaps the biggest change in her life had been learning to shift into a bear, a transformation that had been easier than she'd expected. Kalan had been so patient, explaining how to connect with her inner bear that when she started running, it was as if she'd been born to shift. Sure, her bones cracked, and for a few seconds she couldn't see, but both Izzy and Kalan had explained that would happen, so Elana hadn't been afraid.

Her body adapted quickly to the lumbering movement. In fact, she felt more in control of her body than she ever had in her human form. On that first white moon when she shifted, he'd remained in his human form, clapping and grinning like a fool.

Curious what she looked like as a bear, Elana remembered running up to the house to look in a mirror only to realize she couldn't open the door. Kalan had rushed up to her to see what she was doing. When she telepathed what she wanted to do, he made her stay outside while he retrieved her hand mirror from the bathroom. Later he told her, he feared she might have wrecked the furniture.

Once she took a look, she was a little disappointed that she was a lot smaller than Kalan. Her fur was darker than his, and her snout had an upturn to it whereas Kalan's was rather straight. All in all, she thought she looked cute.

Not being *just* a human anymore made her feel special, and she owed it all to Kalan. The whole concept of her being the Beta's mate, however, had yet to sink in. She knew little about wolves and not much more about bears before meeting him, but she was willing to learn.

"Ready?" Kalan said, coming out from the bedroom looking as hot as ever. His jeans hugged his muscular thighs, and he had on a forest green form-fitting long-sleeved shirt that accentuated his beautiful eyes.

Even though this was Sunday dinner at his parents, she'd dressed casually, as would the rest of his family. If this had been like the ones at her parents' house, she'd have worn a dress, heels, and done up her hair. If nothing else, her parents had drilled into her how to present herself properly. But the Murdochs didn't seem to care about that. To them, family was their number one concern, and they wanted everyone to feel comfortable and relaxed. Sure, they expected excellence from their children, and as far as she could tell, they got it, but they didn't dwell on outward appearances.

When they arrived, Kalan's father, Daniel, greeted them both with a huge hug. Felicia, Kalan's mom, rushed up to them, hugging them as well, and giving them each a peck on the cheek. "Blair had to go into work at the clinic. She said she had to cover for someone, but that she'd be back for dinner. Come on in."

Kalan's mom was the sweetest woman alive, but she was no pushover. From the way she listened to every word, no one could get anything past her. According to his mom, slouches were not acceptable. Elana hoped she could run her household the same way.

Their home was a large two-story house with well-worn comfortable furniture. Mr. Murdoch returned to his lounger while

Kalan's mom hustled into the kitchen.

"Can I help?" Elana asked.

"No dear, go talk with the men."

Kalan's brother Jackson was there. He had such a carefree attitude that would make one think he was younger than her, but in reality he was a year older. Fair-haired with a short beard, he was almost as good-looking as Kalan. Along with Rye's brother, Connor, Jackson worked at McKinnon Security and Associates, and seemed to love his job.

Elana sat next to Kalan on the sofa and Jackson sat in the large chair next to them. "Kalan said you've learned to shift. How was that?" Jackson asked.

She was surprised by the question. "You can shift. Isn't it the same?"

"Probably, but I can't remember the first time since I was only two or three. For me, it just happened. Since you were born a human, it might be different."

"Since I don't know what it's like for you, it's hard to say, but I do love it. The freedom it has given me has changed my life."

Jackson grinned. "Did Kalan tell you that as a shifter you can heal quicker and live longer, along with a host of other wonderful attributes?"

She looked over at Kalan. *"Why didn't you tell me I could do all that?"* she telepathed, her new favorite pastime.

He grinned. *"I've been busy trying to keep you from ripping my clothes off at every turn,"* he answered.

"You are so full of it."

"Children," Felicia said. "Communicating telepathically is the same as bringing a cell phone to dinner and checking your messages."

"Ouch, Mom. Give her a break. I kind of forgot to fill in Elana on all the ins and outs of being a *Were*."

"I thought I raised you better," she said, clearly enjoying sparring with her son.

"I'm sorry, Felicia. I won't do it again. If Kalan telepaths something to me, I'll ignore him."

His mom smiled. "That's what I do to Dan, isn't it sweetheart?" She ruffled Mr. Murdoch's hair and he waved away her hand with a grunt. As she turned away, he reached out and swatted her backside, giving her a big smile.

A phone rang and Felicia rushed to answer it in the kitchen. While Elana's hearing was now sharp enough to pick up what was said, she blocked it out since the call was none of her business. Elana leaned back and drank in all the love in the room. Even though the Bertas were like real parents to her, they weren't as outwardly open as Kalan's family.

Felicia came out of the kitchen wiping her hands on her apron. "I'm afraid Blair has to work a little longer and said we should start without her."

Elana jumped up, wanting to help. This time Kalan's mom didn't shoo her away. Once in the kitchen, Felicia instructed her on what to take out and where to place it. When the meal was ready, the men moved over to the table.

Before they began, Dan Murdoch raised his glass. "To my son and his wonderful mate. May the two of you enjoy your reign over the Clan."

Elana doubted she'd be making any Clan decisions, but perhaps with time she could help Kalan with his.

All during dinner, they regaled her with some of Kalan's antics growing up, including his love of shifting into a bear when he was just a kid and destroying many family heirlooms along the way. She could see why he didn't want her in the house in her bear form.

"We know," Felicia said, "that when we have grandchildren running around here, they won't be able to break anything because there's nothing left to break."

"Mom, I wasn't that bad," Kalan said with an exaggerated frown.

Everyone laughed, but Elana could feel the heat race up her face. It was too soon to be talking about children, but at in the future she wanted some.

Halfway through dinner, Blair arrived. "Sorry I'm late everyone. I got a call from my college roommate."

"Ainsley?" her mom asked.

"Yes. She applied at the clinic where I work and has an interview later this month. She wanted to know if she could crash at my place."

"That's wonderful," Kalan's mom said.

Once Blair was seated, Elana pummeled her with a ton of questions about her job since she found Blair's work at the clinic fascinating.

As soon as they finished eating, Kalan pushed back his chair first and stood. "Elana and I need to be going. I promised her a evening romp."

If she hadn't been looking forward to it for days, she would have insisted they stay. Kalan had worked late several nights in a row and being in her bear form was the most exciting time of her life—other than when she was in bed with him.

They said their goodbyes and then walked back home. Halfway there, her cell rang. It was Izzy. Her friend usually didn't call on a Sunday since she knew they'd be at Kalan's parents' house.

"Go ahead and take it," he said.

She answered. "Hey. What's up?"

"Teagan and Kip broke up again."

"Oh no." Elana wasn't really surprised as there had been tension brewing between them for quite a while.

"She's hurting right now, so don't call her tonight. Plus, she'll know I told you. Tomorrow if you have time, maybe you can check up on her. Now that I'm teaching, I won't be able to get away."

"Sure no problem."

"So how was dinner?" Izzy asked, her tone switching from highly concerned to friendly.

"Awesome. Kalan and I just finished and are about to go for a run."

She squealed. "I won't keep you then. Have fun."

She disconnected. As they entered the house, Elana remained sad that Teagan was going through tough times. "Teagan and Kip broke up."

"That's a shame. Do you want to call her?"

"I'll speak with her tomorrow."

He ran a knuckle down her cheek. "Then let's change."

Not wanting to shred their clothes when they shifted, they always undressed first. As soon as Elana finished removing her shirt, Kalan pressed up against her.

"I know I promised we'd go out, but how about a quickie?"

She wasn't going to be deterred. "Run first, play later."

He tapped her nose. "Spoilsport."

She was naked before Kalan and took off, thinking he wouldn't be able to catch her this time. She rushed out the back sliding glass door and down the porch steps. The half moon was visible in the clear sky, and with summer finally coming to an end, the air was deliciously cool. Kalan could shift in a heartbeat, but she still needed a few seconds of running and concentrating before changing into her bear form.

Without further trying to, Elana was on all fours running and twirling. She dipped her head and did a roll. As if he could perform magic, Kalan was suddenly beside her.

He ran a few circles around her then scrambled up a tree. Elana had enough of tree climbing as a human and wasn't interested in losing her balance and falling even as a bear. Someday she might be brave enough to try.

"Bet you can't catch me," she telepathed to Kalan who was edging his way out on a limb.

"You won't even get halfway to the house before I nab you."

He was so easy to goad into doing something. Elana roared, though the sound wasn't nearly as deep as when Kalan did it, but she was still learning. Before he had the chance to climb down the tree, she took off as fast as her short legs could manage.

Seconds later, Kalan darted in front of her. Man, he was fast. Now was her chance. Her favorite thing was to jump on him especially she was quite small compared to him. He told her because she was short as a human, she'd be a smaller sized bear.

Before he even slowed, she leapt up and landed on his back then kicked his flanks as if he were a horse. Kalan actually lumbered forward instead of stopping. She then shifted into her human form and hung on tight.

"*You will pay for that. You know the rule.*" Kalan lifted up a little before dropping down on all fours.

Ah yes, *the rule*. She was only allowed to ride him if they were both human, naked and in their bed. Elana laughed and hung on tighter. "*You can take it out in trade.*"

"*Then let's get you to bed and enforce that rule!*"

Life as a bear couldn't be better.

Epilogue

"QUIET." BROTHER JACOB pounded the gavel on the wooden table, unhappy the Council was unable to enter without talking. Once they were settled, he held up the knife with the sardonyx blade. "After searching long and hard, we have procured the prized piece of stone from another vendor. This beauty will help rebuild our kind. Brother Arnold did a masterful job of carving the stone into a blade so sharp that it will take little effort to exact the Wendayan's magic."

One of the Council members raised his hand and lowered his face in deference. "Yes, Brother Thomas? You may speak," Brother Jacob said.

"Which magic are we going after? We need many kinds."

"We do indeed. I have spent some time among the Wendayans. They are such a trusting group. After much searching, I have found the perfect man. His name is Landon. Once we extract his abilities to control electricity, we shall be able to do much damage to the shifters."

"That's excellent, Brother Jacob. Simply excellent."

The End

I hope you enjoyed Kalan and Elana's story. To keep up-to-date on my releases, enter contests, and receive some books for free, sign up for my newsletter:

http://eepurl.com/U1dm1

Next up is Teagan and Kip's story—Surge Of Magic. Below is the first chapter!

Chapter One

MASSAGE THERAPIST, TEAGAN Pompley, lit the incense in a back room at the Crystal Winds Spa then opened a bottle of oil in preparation for her next client. As she placed it on the warming plate, her vision suddenly turned black and her body shook. No! No! Not again. She desperately tried to keep the dark images from invading her mind.

Grabbing onto the table for balance, her stomach rolled as the movie swam in front of her eyes. The scent of incense intensified, and the sticky sweet aroma of the open jar of oil made her throat tighten.

With her free hand, Teagan pressed her palm over her left eye and then her right to ease the ache, but even that didn't help lessen the tension. In her vision, she saw herself standing next to Kip, her former boyfriend, and in the next frame, he was swimming in a pool of blood—his blood. Teagan tried to search the scene for clues, but it was as if they were in some kind of white vacuum.

Before she could figure out what was going on, a sharp pain stabbed her arm, and without thinking, she released her grip on the table to clasp her forearm. Her knees gave way and she dropped to the floor, sending an ache ricocheting up her body. A second later, glass splintered next to her, the shards pinging on the tile floor. Then pounding footsteps came near.

The door opened followed by a hand to her back. "Teagan, Teagan! Are you okay?"

No, she wasn't okay. If she were, she wouldn't be on her hands and knees shaking uncontrollably with sweat beading on her forehead. Warmth suffused her body from Missy's touch, and when Teagan's vision slowly cleared she dropped back on her haunches, her breath coming out too fast. "I had another vision."

"Was it of Kip?" her cousin asked.

Teagan had a premonition a few weeks ago about him, but she hadn't been able to determine the extent of the tragedy—only that it was bad. "Yes. I saw him covered in blood."

"What else?"

Teagan shook her head. "That was all. The evil was so intense."

Her cousin threw her arms around her, and her healing comfort helped. "I'm sorry. After I find something to clean up the glass, I'll get you something to drink. Stay right here." She sat back up.

She glanced to the mess. *Shit.* "I must have pushed the table into the counter with the crystals. I'm so sorry." She wasn't ready to tell Missy that the table hadn't moved. Her anger at having another vision had caused the telekinetic reaction, which knocked the glass off the table. Missy's sister, Izzy, was aware of this new power, but Teagan didn't want to tell anyone else until she learned to control it.

"Accidents happen. At least it's replaceable."

As soon as Missy stepped out of the small back room, her cousin took her healing powers with her, and Teagan wanted to vomit. Of late, her visions had been coming more frequently, and each time, it expended more and more of her energy. Her head still pounded and the ache in her chest made it hard to breathe.

A few minutes later, Missy returned from the shop and handed her a cup of water from the cooler. "Here."

With shaky hands, Teagan sipped the liquid. "I can't take this anymore."

Missy swept up the broken glass then dumped the pieces into the trash bin. She then sat next to her on the floor. "Maybe you should warn Kip."

"No. If I call him, I'll want to be with him, and if we're together the event will happen." Only a few times in the past had she been able to alter the future, and she was determined to do so again.

"Then I'll be the one to tell him he needs to be careful," Missy said with compassion.

She grabbed her cousin's arm. "You can't say anything. If Kip knows I had a vision, it will give him an excuse to see me, and I don't think I'm strong enough to stay away. It's better if he thinks I'm not interested."

Missy rubbed Teagan's arm. "You have to tell him the truth."

"If I do, he might end up dead."

Missy looked off to the side then returned her gaze to her. "Your visions don't always come true. Besides, you've been miserable without him."

Her visions did always come true, unless she helped change things. "The pain of losing him would be much worse."

The bell above the store entrance chimed and Missy stood, brushing back wisps of her long auburn hair. "That's probably Mrs. Rodriguez. Do you want me to ask her to reschedule her massage?"

"No, I'll take her. Give me a few minutes to compose myself though. Working on her might keep my mind off what happened."

Once Missy left, Teagan tried to pull herself together. Needing to prepare for her client, she straightened the massage table and tried to smooth out the sheets, but her hands were shaking so much she wasn't sure if she was making things better.

When her client stepped into the small room, Teagan painted on a happy face. For the next forty-five minutes, she would attempt to focus on her job and not on the upcoming tragedy.

The slow rubbing with the oil and the soft music helped reduce her anxiety, but she had to concentrate to keep from worrying about

Kip. When Teagan finished, she pulled the sheet high onto Mrs. Rodriguez's back.

"Rest for a minute and then change. I'll meet you out front."

"Thank you," Mrs. Rodriguez answered, face down on the table.

Teagan stepped into the main room to wait for her client. After Mrs. Rodriguez emerged, looking neat and relaxed, she paid and made another appointment for next month. Needing to clean up her room, Teagan returned to the back, enjoying the solitude for a few more minutes. Somewhere between the time of her vision and finishing the massage, she'd made up her mind about what she needed to do.

For the last few months, almost all of her premonitions had resulted in either someone she cared about being in danger or in pain. The one exception involved Missy's sister, Izzy. Recognizing that something bad was happening at that moment had saved her cousin's life. When the visions about Kip had started, Teagan couldn't chance he'd be taken from her. It seemed that those closest to her were being punished for some deed she must have committed in the past. It was time to break that link, and that meant Teagan had to stay away from everyone she loved.

Once she replaced the linens on the table in her massage room, and extinguished the incense, she went in search of her aunt to ask for some time off. "Where's Aunt Kathryn?" she asked Missy.

"Mom had to make a house call."

That wasn't unusual, but the timing couldn't have been worse. "The store closes in an hour and since no one is scheduled for any treatments for the rest of the day, would you mind if I went home early? I'm not feeling well." That wasn't a lie.

Missy hugged her. "Sure. Take off whatever time you need. You have vacation time that's been stacking up."

"I know, but I don't want to make more work for you. However, if I don't take a few days to clear my head, I won't be much good to anyone."

"Totally. I'll let Mom know." Missy's cell rang and she checked the called ID then looked up. "Oh, no. It's Kip."

Her heart jammed in her throat. "Why would he be calling you?"

Many of the Wendayans and shifters needed Missy's healing powers, but Teagan refused to believe Kip had been injured. Her vision indicated she would be with him when harm struck. Regardless of her belief in her premonitions, her insides cramped thinking Kip could be in need.

"He might be asking why you won't return his calls," Missy suggested.

"We broke up. Or rather I told him I didn't want to date anymore." Teagan's shoulders slumped and tears brimmed on her lids. "You need to answer it but don't tell him what just happened."

"Okay." Missy swiped a finger across the screen. "Hello?" Her skin paled and she held up a finger, indicating Teagan should stay. "Slow down, Kip. Tell me exactly what happened." Her brows furrowed and Teagan's anxiety ramped up. "What's his room number? Don't worry, I'll be right over." She disconnected then faced Teagan. "Two masked men just stabbed Randy."

Kip's twin brother. Teagan's heart nearly jumped out of her chest and she absently rubbed her left arm where she'd experienced the ache. "Is Randy okay?" She waved a hand as if to erase her comment. "That was a stupid question. He wouldn't be in a hospital if he were. Did Kip say how seriously he was hurt?"

"Kip just said Randy called him and told him two men broke into the house, took a few punches him, and then stabbed him." Missy stood. "I'm going to the hospital to see if I can help with the healing. Do you want to come?"

When her friend's brother's hotel room had been broken into recently, two masked men had been responsible. She would have concluded the two incidences were connected, except that one of the intruders had been caught and the other killed. "I can't."

Missy rushed over to the locked cabinet behind the counter and withdrew her flowered bag that contained her herbs, candles, and crystals for healing. "What should I tell Kip then? He'll ask about you."

She didn't want to hurt his feelings, but telling him the truth would be worse. "Maybe say I already went home."

"You're my cousin, and I love you, but I won't lie for you."

She was right. It wasn't fair to ask her. "Tell him I didn't want to be in the way and that someone had to mind the store. You go ahead and help. I'll lock up if Aunt Kathryn doesn't make it back by five."

Missy hugged her again. "He needs you, Teagan."

Guilt swamped her. "Kip will be okay. He has to focus on helping his brother, not on why I've pulled away."

Missy nodded, clasped her bag then rushed out. The moment Missy left, the air seemed thinner and her chest caved. More than anything, she wanted to be with Kip, but to do so could jeopardize his life.

KIP WAS FRANTIC, and it wasn't because his brother had his arm cut open. With a few stiches, the wound would heal, and the bruising on his face and hand would fade with time. It was what Randy had just confided in him that had his panic button pushed.

Kip looked behind him to make sure the curtain to the small emergency room cubicle was closed. Randy was hooked up to monitors that thankfully showed normal readings. "What do you mean you have no powers?"

"Just what it sounds like." Randy held up his uninjured hand like Kip had seen his twin do so many times before. With his fingers extended, he narrowed the tips to the size of a half dollar then aimed at the metal chair across the room. Instead of an electric blast coming from his hand, the overhead light flickered briefly. Normally, the chair would have jumped from the current sizzling through it, scorch marks marring its surface. "See?"

Kip's heart nearly broke at the pain radiating off his twin. A Wendayan losing his magic would be tantamount to a *Were* not being able to shift. If Kip could donate half of his abilities to Randy he would.

Not wanting any nurse or doctor to overhear his conversation, Kip pulled the chair closer to Randy's bed. "Tell me exactly what happened. I don't understand how someone could *steal* your magic right from your arm." The whole concept scared the shit out of him.

Randy rested his uninjured forearm across his pasty forehead. Blood was caked above his right eye from a small cut, and his short dark hair was mussed. Randy's red eyes spoke of too much stress, and the bruise on his cheek and knuckles implied his brother had fought back.

"I was working at my office desk when someone knocked on our front door. I answered it, and when I saw two men wearing masks, I tried to close it, but they barged in anyway."

"Why didn't you check the peephole? It's why it's there." Damn, now wasn't the time to chastise his brother for being careless.

Randy blew out a breath. "I had my mind on my case. Besides, we live in the fucking Cove—a place where crime rarely happens."

"Sorry, go on."

"They smashed their way in, and before I had a chance to zap them, the taller of the two pinned me down while the second man waved a knife. I was able to break the big man's hold and put up a fight for a few seconds, as evidenced by the bruises on my knuckles and face, but in the end they overpowered me."

Fuck. The mere thought of the anger and panic ripping through his brother had Kip's stomach in knots. "Did you do some damage to them?" Kip worked at McKinnon and Associates, a private investigation firm. "If you bruised one of the men, the attacker might be easier to spot."

Randy lifted a shoulder. "Hard to say since they wore their masks. I did manage to kick the one of them in the gut, spin around, and then land a punch to the tall one's face before they took me down again. That's when the shorter guy sliced open my arm."

Kip dragged a hand down his scruffy jawline and blew out a

breath. This was bad. Real bad. "Did they say what they are after?" Perhaps the thugs could be identified by their accent or the deepness of their voices.

"No. Not a word. They came in, tackled me, and cut my arm. They didn't make any demands or attempt to take anything."

Kip wasn't convinced the men had really stolen Randy's magic. The fear of being attacked might have caused some kind of mental block. With time, he hoped Randy's abilities would return. If Kip brought up that theory now, given the strength of his brother's conviction, it would piss him off.

Kip slumped back against his chair. "How did you know again that they stole your magic? They could have been there for some kind of retribution. You do deal with the criminal element." Until last year, Kip had been right beside his brother at the law office. It was one reason why he decided to give up practicing law and join a security team.

"Right after the beefier one stabbed me, he pulled out the knife and ran. Just as he and his partner reached the door, I lifted my good arm with the intention of sending a few hundred volts of electricity through them, only nothing happened."

Kip studied Randy wondering if maybe the blade had been dipped in a strong paralytic or something. "I'm not seeing it. How exactly did they *take* your magic? Fuck, I didn't even think it was possible."

"I know, right? I'm still trying to figure it out."

"I'd say they might have mistaken you for me, but with my short beard and longer hair, they wouldn't have mixed up the two of us." When Kip left the law firm, he let his hair grow and swore he'd never wear another tie again.

"I agree."

"No one runs into a house, stabs the person, and then leaves, especially if he wanted you dead. In the ten years I was at the Public Defender's office, I never heard of any criminal acting that strangely."

"Strange or not, that's what happened."

"I'm going to do my best to find the bastards." He leaned forward. "You sure you didn't piss off any clients?" Randy worked on the side of the prosecution.

"Of late, I've been dealing with some lowlife thugs, but I can't imagine anyone caring what happened to them."

Some piece was missing. "Can you describe the knife?" Kip wasn't even sure why he asked, but there had to be some explanation. Kip had heard stories as a kid about Wendayans losing their magic, but he thought those were just stories. He figured the witches had lost their powers due to old age.

Randy slowly lowered his arm and his gaze shifted to the left. "It had a red blade, but why should that matter? Or more importantly, why use something other than steel? I will say it was damned sharp."

"I have no idea. There has to be a connection as to why you were targeted."

Before Randy could answer, the curtain parted. It was Missy. "Kip?"

He jumped up from his seat. "Hey, thanks for coming by."

Her smile looked like she was having a hard time staying positive. Her auburn hair was pulled back in a ponytail, but many of the strands had come loose. She nodded then rushed over to Randy and set her flowered bag on the bed. "How are you feeling?"

Randy glanced up to him. They were all Wendayans and aware of each other's powers. "I'm going to tell her everything. Missy might be able to shed some light on the situation." Kip nodded. Randy explained what happened, leaving out no details.

"Do you think your powers were transferred to them when they hit you?"

Kip hadn't thought of that possibility.

"I don't think so. If they'd taken something as valuable as my ability to control electricity, they would have used that power against me right away. By all rights, I should be dead. Not that I can identify them, but I will hunt them down."

His brother's face was red and a fleck of blood appeared on the bandage. "Hey, you need to rest. I'll do the looking." Besides, if they didn't get what they came for the first time, they might return, and Randy was in no shape to handle another attack.

"Fine, but take Connor and Jackson with you. These men meant business."

Connor McKinnon and Jackson Murdoch also worked at the private investigation firm with him. The fourth member, Devon McKinnon, mostly ran the branch office. As much as Kip wanted Missy to start her healing ways, he had to find out about Teagan. He faced her. "Does Teagan know what happened to Randy?"

Missy glanced away. "Yes."

That wasn't good. He wasn't one to beg, but he needed to find out why she hadn't come. Teagan was one of the most caring women in the world, and yet in a flash, she'd turned from being wonderful to standoffish in a flash. Something had to have happened for her to announce that she didn't want to see him anymore. "Did she say if she would stop by?"

"No."

He needed to speak with Teagan. "Do you know why she won't return my calls? I know we argued that last night about her visions and how much they are messing with her mind, but that's not a good reason to up and leave a relationship. What we had was good."

Missy pulled out a small burlap sac from her bag. "I've asked, but she won't say."

Now wasn't the time to interrogate Missy—not when his brother needed her help. "Thanks. I appreciate all you can do." Maybe she could pull a miracle out of her bag and bring back his powers.

She placed a sac under Randy's head. "Close your eyes."

Her calm and caring manner was similar to how Teagan had been until the night of their big fight.

Kip vowed that as soon as he brought the men who robbed his brother of his magic to justice, he'd win over Teagan Pompley—no matter what it took.

HIDDEN REALMS OF SILVER LAKE (Paranormal)
Awakened By Flames (book 1)—FREE
Seduced By Flames (book 2)
Kissed By Flames (book 3)
Destiny In Flames (book 4)
Hidden Realms Box Set (books 1-4)
Passionate Flames (book 5)
Ignited By Flames(book 6)

FOUR SISTERS OF FATE: HIDDEN REALMS OF SILVER LAKE (Paranormal)
Poppy (book 1)
Primrose (book 2)
Acacia (book 3)
Magnolia (book 4)
Box Set (books 1-4)

WERES AND WITCHES OF SILVER LAKE (Paranormal)
A Magical Shift (book 1)
Catching Her Bear (book 2)
Surge of Magic (book 3)
The Bear's Forbidden Wolf (book 4)
Box Set(books 1-4)
Her Reluctant Bear (book 5)
Freeing His Tiger (book 6)
Protecting His Wolf (book 7)
Waking Her Bear (book 8)
Box Set (books 5-8)
Melting Her Wolf's Heart (book 9)
Her Wolf's Guarded Heart (book 10)
His Rogue Bear (book 11)

PACK WARS (Paranormal)—**BUY OR READ ON KU**
Training Their Mate (book 1)—FREE

Claiming Their Mate (book 2)
Rescuing Their Virgin Mate (book 3)
Box Set (books 1-3)
Loving Their Vixen Mate (book 4)
Fighting For Their Mate (book 5)
Enticing Their Mate (book 6)
Box Set (books 1-4)
Complete Box Set (books 1-6)

HIDDEN HILLS SHIFTERS (Paranormal)
An Unexpected Diversion (book 1)-FREE
Bare Instincts (book 2)
Shifting Destinies (book 3)
Box Set (books 1-3)
Embracing Fate (book 4)
Promises Unbroken (book 5)
Bear 'N Dirty (book 6)
Hidden Hills Shifters Complete Box Set (books1-6)

MONTANA PROMISES (Full length contemporary)—**BUY OR READ ON KU**
Promises of Mercy (book 1)
Foundations For Three (book 2)
Montana Fire (book 3)
Montana Promises Box Set (books 1-3)
Hart To Hart (Book 4)
Burning Seduction (Book 5)
Montana Promises Complete Box Set (books 1-5)

ROCK HARD, MONTANA (contemporary novellas)
Montana Desire (book 1)
Awakening Passions (book 2)

PLEDGED TO PROTECT (contemporary romantic suspense)—**BUY OR READ ON KU**
From Panic To Passion (book 1)
From Danger To Desire (book 2)
From Terror To Temptation (book 3)
Pledged To Protect Box Set (books 1-3)

BURIED SERIES (contemporary romantic suspense)—**BUY OR READ ON KU**
Buried Alive (book 1)
Buried Secrets (book 2)
Buried Deep (book 3)
The Buried Series Complete Box Set (books 1-3)

A NASH MYSTERY (Contemporary)—**BUY OR READ ON KU**
Sidearms and Silk(book 1)
Black Ops and Lingerie(book 2)
A Nash Mystery Box Set (books 1-2)

STARTER SETS
Contemporary—**BUY OR READ ON KU**
Paranormal

STANDALONES
A Billionaire's Roar

Author Bio

Want a FREE book? Sign up for my newsletter and receive free books.
COPY AND PASTE INTO YOUR BROWSER:
https://app.mailerlite.com/webforms/landing/i1e8b2

Check out my latest interview on You Tube:
http://youtube.com/sQo5pyyVMDI

Not only do I love to read, write, and dream, I'm an extrovert. I enjoy being around people and am always trying to understand what makes them tick. Not only must my books have a happily ever after, I need characters I can relate to. My men are wonderful, dynamic, smart, strong, and the best lovers in the world (of course).

I believe I am the luckiest woman. I do what I love and I have a wonderful, supportive husband, who happens to be hot!

Fun facts about me

(1) I'm a math nerd who loves spreadsheets. Give me numbers and I'll find a pattern.
(2) I love photography, so I'll be posting pictures—especially of my Costa Rican adventure.
(3) I also like to exercise. Yes, I know I'm odd. Not only do I lift weights, I love to hike and walk on the beach (yes, it sounds like an ad for a date)

I love hearing from readers either on FB or via email (hint, hint).

Social Media Sites

Website:
www.velladay.com

FB:
facebook.com/vella.day.90

Twitter:
@velladay4

Gmail:
velladayauthor@gmail.com

Google:
plus.google.com/u/0/116041077486216602121/posts

Instagram:
@dayvella

Made in the USA
Columbia, SC
22 March 2024